CAESAR

A NOVEL BY MICHAEL COLE

SEVERED**PRESS**

CAESAR

Copyright © 2023 by MICHAEL COLE

WWW.SEVEREDPRESS.COM

All rights reserved. No part of this book may be reproduced or transmitted in any form or by any electronic or mechanical means, including photocopying, recording or by any information and retrieval system, without the written permission of the publisher and author, except where permitted by law.

This novel is a work of fiction. Names, characters, places and incidents are the product of the author's imagination, or are used fictitiously. Any resemblance to actual events, locales or persons, living or dead, is purely coincidental.

ISBN: 978-1-922861-83-2

CHAPTER 1

Dr. John Kerr held his breath and held still. He could feel the layers of granite shifting beneath his feet as the angry planet shook. Of all the times to explore this rare spherical gem, it had to be when the tectonic plates were beginning to shift and reshape its underwater landscape.

From the naked eye, RP-275 was a paradise. Draped in clear blue waters, with oxygen richer than the green days of Earth, it was sure to be a popular vacation spot and retirement home. For the most part, it was an ocean planet with small stretches of land scattered throughout. Some were made entirely of rock, while others flourished with bright green fauna that gifted RP-275 with oxygen.

Discovered seven standard years ago, the planet was immediately sought after by the United Assembly. It was not just the abundance of water they craved, but the potential resources beneath the crust.

John was bummed to find that his research mission would be based on one of the rocky islands. Regardless, he still considered himself lucky. He was among the first to set foot on this world and breathe in its clean, salty air. Alas, the planet did not feel the same way. It was shaking with rage, as though repulsed by their very presence.

Even after five calls to headquarters, John Kerr was unable to get permission to evacuate his small crew. Every conversation garnered the same response. "Just seismic activity," the Assembly representative said, "No big deal. Just tough through it. Continue with the research." A typical brainless government liaison. John had looked into the man's credentials. Four years, with middling grades, at a sub-par college in Utah. Following that, he worked for five years managing a boot factory until becoming a regional lieutenant governor's assistant. After four years of that, he was promoted to Sector 75, working for the administration there. Zero education and work history regarding scientific research.

John was not the type to look down on other people and their careers, unless he was expected to answer to that person.

It was after the southwest end of the island broke away when John made his sixth call. The flattest part of the island, where the shuttle was docked, broke away, burying their only transport in the seabed. The ocean was swallowing this island little by little. Given enough time, he and his crew would be swallowed with it. So much for paradise.

Finally, the request was granted. Now, all he had to worry about was getting everyone prepped for evac... and hope the island would hold together long enough for pickup to arrive.

John stood outside Smith Station, holding his breath as the tremors began to die down.

"Whoa!" Trace Melbourne, the outpost Engineering supervisor, had his hands held out to keep balance. "Thought that was gonna be the big one for a moment there."

Andre Llosa, his only staff member, approached from the docks. "You feel that?"

"Nah, of course not," John Kern said.

His sarcasm was not lost on the outpost staff. Andre chuckled, partly out of relief that the island was still intact. Still, he was glancing about to make sure. The northeast radio tower up on the hill was still there. The generators were in place, as were the secondary dock and drone charging stations on the east shores. Given the rate of decay, those structures were on borrowed time.

Smith Station's main facility was a single-story building, resembling an oversized mobile home from the late Twentieth Century, except built with more advanced technology. Its back half was almost entirely a laboratory, the front section divided into crew quarters, communications room, the cafeteria, and lounge.

"What's the word on pickup?" Trace asked.

"Finally got that pencilneck to let us get the hell out of here," John said. "There's a freighter coming out of Sector 74. Personnel vessel from Rosseni. Should pass within range in a couple of days. Its computer will wake up a rescue to come get us."

"Thank God," Andre said. He patted his cargo pants, the black fabric looking grey from all of the sediment coming off the rocks. Nobody on this island had a set of clothes that hadn't been touched by the island. The rocks were covered by tiny particles that clung like dust to anything that touched them. Even John Kerr's black boots showed no sign of their original color. It was the same for the drones and mechanical equipment.

"Where's Sara?" John asked.

"Dr. McQuade?" Andre said. He was always formal when addressing the professors, even behind their backs. Even though John and Sara felt they were on a first-name basis with everyone here, it was always "Dr. Kern" and "Dr. McQuade" when it came to Andre. He turned southeast, put his hand over his eyes, then pointed to the shore beyond the hill. "I saw her head out that way."

"Good," John said. "She's probably checking the driller. We gotta retrieve all of the samples we can before pickup. And the microchips... Oh! By the way..."

"Yeah, yep-yep-yep-yep-yep-yep-yep," Trace said, waving his hand dismissingly. He already knew what instruction John was going to relay from 'Pencilneck'. "Gotta retrieve all microchips from the machinery. Already on it. Come on, Andre. Let's start with the boats and the sub."

The two Engineers went northeast, pausing momentarily as another small aftershock swept underneath the island.

"Jeez," Andre muttered. "To think I was considering retiring to this place..."

"Hopefully it's a temporary thing, because I'm still clinging to hope," Trace said. They hiked over the island's rocky exterior, leaving John standing near the facility entrance.

From here, he had a direct view to the west shoreline. The water crashed into the shallows, gradually calming down. After a few moments, the ocean was clear and gentle again, until the next earthquake riled it up again.

Me too, guys. Me too.

He forced the fantasy from his mind and hustled southeast to find Sara.

***

A blue translucent light stretched from the scanner and swept over the soft, wet flesh. Sara panned the device back and forth in her third attempt to solve the strange mystery lying in front of her.

Rigid pectoral fins, a cone-shaped jaw, and some rib bones and spinal column was all that remained of the large hazerfish. Sara had ruled this new species as the killer whales of RP-275. Judging by the remains, in life, this specimen was a thirty-five-foot male. Up until now, she believed it to be one of the dominant species in the ocean. Generally, they hunted in packs, using team efforts to bring down large prey. Their teeth grew up to four inches and could pierce light metal. It was not a creature to be messed with, making its death all the more mysterious. Either it died of natural causes and was devoured by scavengers, or it encountered something worse—something that the rest of its pack could not defend it from.

"Ah, there you are."

Sara looked over her left shoulder. "Hi, John."

He chuckled as he descended the small, granite hill. "Even as the island threatens to plunge, the tenacious Dr. Sara McQuade remains dedicated to her research."

Sara's grin vanished after the device completed its scan. "That's strange…"

"What's the matter?" John asked.

"I'm scanning for teeth marks," Sara said. "I'm trying to see what killed this hazerfish."

John stood over its head, eyeing its parted jaw. "And?"

Sara shrugged. "I can't find any bite wounds." An exasperated sigh followed the statement.

All John could do was chuckle.

"Sara, not all underwater predators have toothed jaws. Perhaps this thing encountered a hawk eel. They're pretty big and they've got them big beaks."

Sara shook her head. "One on one, maybe. But the pack would have made fast work of a hawk eel. Even then, I'd be able to detect a bite radius."

"Well, maybe it died of natural causes and was nibbled by scavengers," John said.

"Maybe."

"You sound disappointed," John said.

Sara stood up. "I don't like unanswered questions."

"That's what makes you an obsessed scientist," John said.

"Not sure if I should take that as a compliment or an insult."

"Just a fact," John said.

Sara smirked. "Perhaps there's truth to that." She turned her eyes to the horizon. Her expression turned sour.

"I'll state another fact," John said, watching her body language. "We'll send probes to the planet and monitor the seismic activity. I'm certain these quakes are a temporary thing. *How temporary* is the real question. When things settle down, I'll be sure to get you reassigned here if you wish."

"Not too many places in the galaxy for a marine biologist," Sara said.

"You're barely that," John said. "You're here as an underwater geologist."

"Surveyer, according to the powers-that-be." Sara shut down the scanning device and clipped it to her belt. Now was not the time for biology research. She knew John did not walk over here just to socialize.

Behind her was the control module for the underwater core sampler. The manufacturers referred to it as a drone driller, a name as lazy as the packaging. So many resources put into complex components to withstand water, corrosion, and depth pressures, yet they literally packed the thing in cardboard and Styrofoam.

"The government man telling us to retrieve all underwater samples?"

John nodded. "Samples. Microchips. Everything that doesn't float will become an underwater relic of Mankind's first visit to this place."

Sara picked up the module and activated it. After a few moments of waking up, the screen lit up, displaying a small map of the region. In the top of the screen was the east side of the island.

"Shouldn't we just take one of the boats out?" Sara asked.

"Normally, I'd say yes," John said. "Now? For all we know, another quake could happen that'll generate waves large enough to flip our boats over. I'm not eager to be the first underwater burial on this planet. Just steer the drones to the shallows."

"Your wish is my command," Sara said. She typed in the command code. A moment later, the words *return to port* appeared on the bottom. The drones retracted their drills, secured their core samples, and initiated their return trip.

***

Trace cursed under his breath. He wasn't sure what was more annoying. The angle in which these screws were placed under the console, or Andre's incessant whistling. His mind could only describe the sound as a dying bird trying to regurgitate its last meal...while drunk.

"Will you knock that shit off so I can concentrate?"

The whistling came to a spitting conclusion. Andre wiped his face, then crossed his arms.

"You just don't appreciate a good tune."

"If you call a parrot getting raped a good tune, then sure." He put the cordless screwdriver to the corner of the panel.

One by one, the screws spiraled from their slots beneath the console, giving Trace access to the mako cruiser's microchip. It was an annoying process to get to it, requiring Trace to get on his back and take an old-fashioned flathead. Some tools never outlived their usefulness.

"I got this one. Go check Boat Three," he said to Andre.

"What about Two?" Andre said, cocking his head toward the adjacent boat. The retired Beluga-class vessel that was Boat Two was docked between One and Three. A retired combat gunboat, it dwarfed its two siblings. Though Boat One and Three had plenty of deck space for the research crews to conduct their work, Boat Two was unofficially chosen as the primary vessel.

"Because Two's microchip is surprisingly easy to access," Trace said. "Three's is a bitch, though. Hence, I'm making you do it. Oh, and after that, I'm gonna make you handle the chip on the submersible." He nodded at the fifteen-foot lime-colored exploratory machine on Boat Two's aft deck.

"Oh, thanks!" Andre said. He hopped off the deck onto the pebbly shore. "Anyone ever tell you you're a swell guy?"

Trace gritted his teeth, fumbling with the flathead screwdriver. "I'd be lying if I said yes."

"At least you're honest."

Andre began whistling his annoying tune again, making sure to keep the pitch loud enough for Trace to hear. Even all the way from Boat Three, the idiot resembled some kind of bird making its death throes.

He worked the first screw free, growling a few curse words after it fell on his face. He went for the next one, his wrist straining as he worked the angle to even tough the flathead to the screw.

All the while, that whistling continued. Tormenting him. Like radio static in his mind, it messed with his concentration. Finally, he could not take it anymore.

"Good lord, dude. Knock it off."

Right then, the whistling concluded with a high-pitched shriek, a gag, then silence… aside from the sound of thumping.

Trace chuckled, waiting for Andre to state whatever caused his sound of fumbling. Probably tripped over a beverage can. The fool had a way of leaving trash about.

"The hell happened to you?" Trace said, smiling. He waited for Andre's response, or worse, for the whistling to continue. Instead, the thumping continued. A new sound reached his ears. A tearing sound, as though Andre's clothing was being ripped off his body.

Trace sat up. He couldn't quite see Boat Three, thanks to Two being in the way.

"Andre? The hell are you doing?"

The sounds continued, with splashing joining the mix. It wasn't simply crashing waves. No, it was precise splashing of water, as though the engineer was wallowing in the shallows.

Trace propped himself up on the console seat. He could just barely see over Boat Two's bow. Several yards past it was Boat Three. Andre was not aboard.

His absence was not nearly as alarming as the sight of his tools. They were scattered on the dock, the toolkit having fallen into the water.

Trace hopped off the boat and sprinted to shore, slowing as he passed Boat Two. The sound took on grotesque characteristics, as though something was being grinded. There was a simultaneous dryness and wetness to the noise, as though soft tissue and solid components were being ground into bits. He had worked in a machine factory during his twenties. It was in his second year when he heard a sound somewhat similar to this. A worker's glove caught in a spinning machine. In an instant, his entire arm was as flexible as a wet noodle, wrapped repeatedly around the shaft. Bone splintered into a hundred pieces and the flesh became pulp.

"Andre?"

There was a slurping sound coming from the other side of Boat Three.

Trace's instincts told him to back away. Despite this, he inched closer, stepping past the bow.

His instincts were right.

He stood silent, beholding the sight of the mess scattered across the shore that minutes ago was Andre Llosa. Intestines, shredded organs, rib bones, spinal columns, hands, feet... his head... were all spread out.

In the middle was a large mass, propped up on eight legs, its hide as rigid as the rocks that made up this island.

Trace froze, his mind in a dispute with itself. He wondered if what he saw was real or if his mind was playing some kind of sick joke.

Alas, it was, in fact, real.

He came to this conclusion a moment too late. When he turned to run, the predator had already lunged.

***

"The hell?"

One moment, John Kern was watching the first drone make its way to the surface. The next, his eyes shot north toward the sound of intense screams. They were coming from the docks. The deep voice was undeniably Trace's. They weren't just screams, but cries of agony, as though his body was being whipped side-to-side.

Sara dropped the module. "What's happening?"

"I don't know."

They sprinted toward the docks. As they went, Ben Cross, the medical officer on site, emerged from the main building's front entrance.

"Is that Trace?"

By now, his screams had descended into squealing, something akin to what one expected to hear in a third-world slaughterhouse.

John and Sara did not provide an answer.

A few short moments later, they arrived at the docks. They came to an abrupt stop. Trace was crawling on the ground, his arms outstretched. He was breathing shallowly, inching himself towards them, his waist smearing blood on the ground.

A few meters behind him were his legs—*parts* of his legs. They had been cut to size. They saw a foot, a shin, part of a thigh.

Standing over them was something that, at first, resembled a large grey rock. Then they noticed the spider-like appendages protruding from its sides, and the two bulky arms that held the juicy fragments of Trace's legs. Their tips, dripping red droplets of blood, opened and shut like scissors. Or pincers.

CHAPTER 2

The adrenaline hit like a bolt of lightning.

Richard Carson awoke from his cryosleep pod and sat up. His heart had gone from a gentle, steady pace to rapid thumping. His chest ached, his nose and throat filled with the gooey residue that built up in the pod. He leaned over the side and dry heaved into the tray. Nothing but a few blue droplets came out.

He immediately knew the space freighter *Banning* had not reached its destination. Had that been the case, he and the other passengers would have to endure the sluggishness of waking up. The computer would only awaken him with an adrenaline shot in the event of an emergency. There was no time for cryosleep fatigue.

As his senses returned to him, he heard his commander's voice echoing through the intercom.

"Squad Bravo-One-Seven, get your gear on and report to Hangar Bay Three."

Richard looked down the row of cryosleep pods. Inside were the staff of Rosseni, RP-268. Engineers, refinery workers, welders, tech staff, medical staff, food prep, grounds workers, marines, teachers, kids—two thousand people at the end of their two-year rotation, dreaming about going home.

Almost all of them were still asleep, oblivious to the announcement that echoed through the compartment. Only the cryosleep chambers that housed the members of Marine Squad Bravo-One-Seven were open.

Several pods down, he saw Quinn leaning over his bin. The medic spat the gooey substance from the back of his throat, then took a few deep breaths while he endured the initial effects of the accelerated wake-up procedure.

"I knew it," he muttered, wiping the crap from his short black hair. "Two years on Rosseni, dealing with brats, overgrown worms, and measly pirate patrols. Everyone bragged about how they're ready to party. Me? I knew going home was too good to be true."

"Oh, quit being such a pussy," said a female Russian voice.

Quinn and Richard looked down the row of pods. Several yards to Quinn's right was Milla Tarasov, the team's heavy weapons specialist. Unlike them, she awoke without a care in the world. Already, she was strutting on the floor in her underwear with a lit cigar clenched in her teeth. Smoking inside a starship was completely against regulations, but Milla didn't care. She was at the end of her stint in the U.A.M.C.

In the next row was Al Jordan, flight pilot. He was sitting up from his cryo pod, grinning as he watched Milla walk toward Corridor C.

"No need for an adrenaline shot when you have that to wake up to," he said.

"Certainly better than looking at your pasty white ass," his co-pilot, Roger Grill, said. Like a wedded couple, their pods were next to each other.

Al wiped his nose, watching Milla disappear into the corridor without a care in the world.

"Definitely better than looking at your blistery face," he said to Roger.

"You're the one who told me the fuel cell had cooled down, dipshit," Roger said. He looked at a small mirror on his pod. The blistering that occurred after his last post-flight inspection was still there. "We haven't been asleep for long."

"No," Quinn said. He hauled himself out of his chamber and stretched. "By the looks of it, we just had a real expensive nap."

"Pilots!" said a husky voice from down the second row of pods. Standing beside his pod was a six-foot-three walking piece of muscle who pointed at Al and Roger. "They woke up dropship pilots. We're leaving the ship."

"Oh, great," Quinn said. "We better get some kind of bonus or some shit."

"Job's technically done when we get back to Earth," Richard said.

All eyes turned to him.

"Ah, they woke you up too, I see, Corporal," Roger said.

Richard was unsure whether he wanted to respond to that. "I am part of Bravo-One-Seven."

Quinn cleared his throat. "At the moment." It was under his breath, but still managed to reach the Corporal's ears.

Richard hauled himself out of his pod. Cryo fluid dripped from his lean figure. The adrenaline in his veins was not helping with his temper. He was already looking at a demotion upon his return to Fort Matthews. Possibly even reassignment. If they kept him in the Corps, he could see the powers-that-be moving him to food service or some kind of desk work on some boring, undesirable location.

"Blech!"

Richard was relieved when everyone's gazes shifted toward Portman's cryo pod. Sure enough, the tattooed-covered infantryman was the only one to actually vomit. Quinn had warned him about having a 'last hurrah' before boarding the vessel.

"Told ya so," the medic said.

"Shut up," Portman muttered. "Ugh… please tell me we've arrived home."

"Yes!" Foreman said. "They totally just awoke the ten of us with an adrenaline shot just to let us know we arrived on Earth."

Portman looked around, then couched into his bin. "Ohhh… come on!"

The Commander's voice echoed through the intercom again.

"Get off your asses, people. Jackman, don't act like you're too sick to work. You're coming too, you lazy prick."

Portman looked to one of the security cameras in the overhead corner. He saluted, knowing he was being watched by Sergeant Lou Walker.

Foreman was heading for the door. "Boss is getting impatient. Better see what's up."

"Where's Stevie and Jac?" Quinn said.

"Knowing them, probably already in the hangar waiting for us," Foreman said. "Let's go, people. Sooner we do this, the sooner we can go back to bed."

Richard shut his eyes. Foreman was looking for a promotion and knew he likely had his spot in the bag. Already, he was acting the part. It seemed to suit him, for the other marines were quick to follow him into the corridor.

Richard waited a few extra moments, dreading the fact that of all squads, it was *his* that had to be woken up for this spur-of-the-moment task. He was ready to wake up and face the music on Fort Matthews. Rip the Band-aid off quick. Get away from his teammates, who, if anything, seemed eager for him to get shipped off somewhere else.

Holding up the mission wasn't going to do himself any favors. Richard entered the hallway and went into the shower rooms. No sense in having this cryo crap all over him during what was likely his last assignment as a United Assembly Marine Corps infantryman.

CHAPTER 3

When Richard arrived in Hangar Bay Three, he saw Al and Roger running the routine diagnostics on the dropship. Fifty feet in length, the vessel was capable of carrying over thirty personnel in addition to four crew members, as well as up to four units of heavy equipment. In this instance, a recovery crane.

The machine didn't look like much at first glance. Made of Barlow steel and designed by Tek-Paru engineers, the relatively small crane proved to punch above its weight. Or in its case, lift. It was already in the cargo hold alongside two large steel cases labeled *Engineering Department.*

"Alright, let's run the scan on engine two," Al said.

"Mind if I finish my coffee first?" Roger said, stumbling across the deck with the hot mug in hand.

Al sniggered, dropping the digital check sheet to his side. "Didn't you just get an adrenaline shot?"

"Wasn't enough," Roger said.

"Nothing's ever enough for you." Al turned to the engine shaft. "Come on. The boss is in a hurry. So am I. I wanna go back to bed and wake up to the pretty sight of Earth."

"If you call a grey desert planet pretty."

"There's still some green in my hometown," Al said. "More people are going off-planet, so that slowed the industrialization of Hawaii."

The two pilots glanced in Richard's direction as he crossed the hangar bay. On the portside of the bay were the offices and conference rooms. He entered a small hallway, then took the first door on the right.

Inside the conference room were a few rows of steel tables and chairs. His fellow marines were already seated and chatting amongst themselves. Milla was halfway through her cigar. Foreman and Quinn were on the right side of the room, both more awake and energized now that the shot was wearing off.

Portman was in the front row, playing up the "I'm sick" act, something the Sergeant was not buying into.

On the front left table were Stevie and Jac.

Stevie turned and gave the Corporal a disparaging glance. His right forearm was still red with scar tissue. The natural color would probably never return. Fortunately, that was the only acid burn injury he'd suffered. Others had gotten it much worse—something Richard would never live down.

Jac was busy staring at the map on the big screen. A man of few words, he preferred to pay attention to detail. Richard had heard his ambition was to be a detective for the U.A. On plenty of occasions, his observation skills were put to use by the Sergeant during missions back on Rosseni, and the mineral planet Vedran before that.

In the front of the room was Sergeant Lou Walker. A warrior with a face seemingly carved from stone, he rarely smiled. His face was scarred where the skin had dried and cracked on Vedran. He never complained when it happened, nor did he ever seem to notice the change in his appearance. A true U.A. marine, his focus was strictly on the job and nothing else. He never got distracted by miniscule and irrelevant details.

"Corporal," he said. Having your name or rank stated was the closest thing to a hello anyone ever got from Walker. The Sergeant stood, hands behind his back, waiting for Richard to take his seat. "Now that we're all here, let's get started."

On the wall behind him was a screen displaying two images. The smaller one showed a planet covered almost entirely in blue ocean. There were a few little dots of land peppered across its surface, some rich in green tropical plants, others clearly grey rock.

Knowing the Assembly, that blue would soon be covered by stretches of black and grey, as monorail systems and residential fortresses were likely already in the planning.

"This here," Walker said, pointing his thumb at the planet, "is Challenger, Registered Planet number two-seven-five."

"We going for a swim, Sarge?" Portman said.

"You might be if you open your mouth again," Walker said. "Seeing as we've all been woken up abruptly, obviously you know we're heading here in a hurry."

He hit a button on the computer, bringing the second image front and center. It was a satellite image of one of the islands. A jagged stretch of land, it was one-and-a-quarter miles from north to south, its width being a little under a mile at its widest point. Markers on the image revealed the components to the settlement located on this island.

On the north side was the outpost facility, stationed beside a garage, maintenance building, and greenhouse. The communications tower was in the northeast corner, which the map indicated as having high elevation. Farther south on the east shore was a separate structure, similar in size to the garage. On the island's southernmost end was the shuttle and a few shacks for the flight crew.

"This is Smith Station," Walker said, aiming a laser pointer at the main facility. "First people to set foot on this planet. Geological survey and some other research, most of which none of you will give a shit about."

Richard felt as though he was about to shrivel into his seat. Had he not been somewhat hazy, he would have recognized the planet outright. Challenger... Smith Station... Dr. Sara McQuade.

Oh, great. Of all the people to go here, why me?

Walker's eyes locked onto him. "Problem, Corporal?"

"No sir," Richard said.

Milla cracked a smile. "Oh boy. Small world, or universe, whichever..." Most of the squad turned, more interested in the dirt she had on Richard than the briefing itself. "His ex was assigned to that planet."

"Wasn't this the mission she took to get away from his sorry ass?" Stevie said.

"That's what I heard," Portman said.

"She's a marine biologist and geologist," Jac added. "Double major. Took the assignment probably because there's not much work in her field in this corner of the universe."

Richard slowly exhaled, relieved that the future detective's attention to detail worked in his favor.

"*And* it probably helped to get her off Rosseni after what happened to her brother," Jac added. "Martin was his name. Nice guy. I remember him... just as much as I remember Private Lowery."

Richard clenched his jaw, the sense of relief replaced with bitterness.

Milla cleared her throat, acknowledging their Sergeant's visible impatience. The squad faced forward, Portman offering an awkward smile at his leader. As usual, the humor was lost on Sergeant Walker.

"For people who are eager to get back in the cryo pods, you sure seem to enjoy wasting time," he said. Returning his attention to the map, he continued the briefing. "As I mentioned, this is Smith Station, probably named after someone with relevance to this subject matter... don't know, don't care. Regardless, it holds nine staff. Two flight personnel, two scientists, a couple assistants, a medical doctor, and two engineers. They've been here roughly six months. Supposed to be a two-year assignment, but they have to stop prematurely due to increased seismic activity on this section of the globe."

"Isn't that what their shuttle's for?" Quinn asked.

"Apparently a section of the island broke away," Walker said. He walked up to the screen and put his finger on the south end where the marker read *shuttle*. "From what I was told, they had an earthquake, and this part of the island broke away, taking their shuttle with it. It might be reparable, might not. Fortunately, we're bringing along two crewmen who will be able to help."

Everyone looked to the doors as two bearded men entered the room. They wore dirty jumpsuits, black boots, and had goggles propped on their foreheads. Both were strong-looking fellas, the darker-skinned one giving vibes of ex-military.

The second man made sure to throw an admiring glance in Milla's direction, which she did not reciprocate.

"Hey."

She did not reciprocate that either.

"Marines, you all remember Jerry Morgalo and Dante Ragsdale."

"They woke you all up too, huh?" Jerry, the darker-skinned engineer said. His fellow staff member, Dante, kept his eyes on Milla. Something about wearing the black combat gear made her look even sexier in his eyes. Jerry elbowed him in the ribs, getting his attention. "Take a seat before she kicks your ass."

"Aw." Dante fell into the nearest chair and tapped his hands on the table. He eyed the eight squad members. "They woke up a bunch of marines for a pickup mission? What else is going on?"

He quieted down after seeing a hard-boiled stare from Walker. Though they weren't military, the engineers still fell under the Sergeant's jurisdiction in this instance. Even if that wasn't the case, Dante knew it would not be long before his boss, Jerry, would have shut him up himself.

Fortunately for Jerry, Sergeant Walker's intimidating demeanor made his job easy. They had encountered him on plenty of occasions back on Rosseni and knew he had no patience for shenanigans.

"Thirty-six hours ago, Dr. John Kerr, the head scientist at Smith Station, got the go-ahead to evacuate," Walker said. "That was the last direct radio contact Fukuda Station received from them, despite repeated attempts to receive updates. Exploration satellites in this region have confirmed pirate activity. Two months ago, they tried to hijack a supply freighter heading towards Nordvark."

"You said thirty-six hours ago was the last direct contact," Richard said. "Was there an intercepted transmission since then?"

Walker simply nodded, his silence conveying an aura of apprehension. On the desk beside him was a recording device. He hit the playback button and let the squad listen to the static-filled message.

"...The tower is disabled. I'm using ... ... on the boat. We... ... ... in the... ... back room. Please, send he—... ..."

It was a female voice, the words broken up by static. Richard straightened his posture, recognizing Sara McQuade's voice. A couple of marines shot glances in his direction. Everyone remained silent. The obvious urgency in the geologist's voice drove home the fact that this possibly may not be a simple in-and-out pickup mission.

"I've completed scans for a two-million-kilometer radius of the planet," Walker said. "There's no sign of any spacecraft in the vicinity, and there's no pirate technology capable of evading our probes. Still, it appears they've run into some kind of trouble. We were awakened as a precautionary measure, but we will treat this as though there's a definite threat down there. As we've learned on Rosseni, pirates are not the only hazard we humans face. There's wildlife, geological threats, possibly even an outpost member gone apeshit for all we know. Could be nothing at all."

"She's using the boat radio," Jac said. "They're equipped with long distance radios. Their signals break up at a shorter distance, hence the static."

"Doesn't explain the fact that she sounds like she's running a marathon," Quinn said.

"Or that she hasn't radioed since, especially now that we're closer," Richard said.

"Earthquake, maybe," Jac said. "Probably damaged the island more. Disabled the tower. Maybe did damage to the boats."

Walker switched off the monitors and tossed the remote down.

"The only way we can know for sure is to go down there and find out. Let's get this done and over with. Gear up and report to the bird in ten."

Without saying another word, Sergeant Walker exited the room and made his way to the armory.

The rest of the squad followed him out, leaving the two engineers at their table, sipping coffee.

"Do I get a gun too?" Dante said.

Jerry laughed. "All you'd do is shoot yourself in the foot."

CHAPTER 4

"Hello ladies!" Portman exclaimed. He was the second one, after Walker, to step into the armory and lay eyes on the beautiful toys at their disposal. He went to the nearest safe which stored over a dozen HK-231 plasma pulse battle rifles. He sorted through the weapons, finding his personalized rifle in the middle. He raised the weapon high, sporting its thick barrel and threaded muzzle.

The Hunter-Killer-231 was intimidating in appearance and especially in execution. With a plasma bolt magazine capacity of fifty-rounds, it was the definitive standard infantry weapon in the service. He looked at his personalized inscription on the frame.

S. P.

"Ah, yes. There it is."

Milla stopped beside him and glanced at the letters. "Small Penis. Yeah, we know." She tapped his shoulder and moved on.

"What?" Portman glanced at the letters, then back at her. "No! It's Scott Portman, you commie bitch."

"Portman," Walker said. "Quit whining about your little dick and gear up."

The infantryman bit his lip. It was the closest thing to humor ever displayed by the Sergeant, and go figure, it was at his expense. The other marines made sure to add to his misery by pointing and laughing like high schoolers.

"Don't worry, Portman," Quinn said. "Every squad has a member with such an issue. In this case, it just happens to be you."

"No wonder he's avoided at the bar," Foreman said.

"Lovely." Portman nodded, letting his teammates have their fun. "Go ahead. Get it out of your systems. Jackasses."

"Aw." Stevie approached the rifle rack and grabbed his own HK-231 plasma rifle. He stood beside Portman and rested an elbow on his shoulder. "Get your facts straight, Marines. Portman doesn't get rejected at *every* bar."

Portman looked down. "Oh, hell…"

Sure enough, the team chuckled in unison. Even Walker had the slightest hint of a smile on his face.

"I heard he got his ass grabbed a ton while he was in there," Foreman said. "Doesn't happen unless you like it!"

"Hey, don't judge," Stevie said, his ridiculous smile stretching across his face.

"Oh, ha-ha." Portman smacked his elbow away, sparking more laughter. "I thought I'd try a different place to drink. I hadn't been there before. I thought, 'hmm, why not?' I didn't know it was a 'special bar', alright."

"You'd think nothing but dudes in skinny jeans would be an indicator," Jac said.

Milla chuckled. "Hell, you'd think the ass grabbing would've been an indicator."

"It was crowded. I didn't know who was doing it. I thought some hottie may have been passing by."

"Oooh!" Stevie pointed. "So, technically, you were enjoying it."

"Not until I realized—oh forget it!" Portman said. He glanced in Richard Carson's direction as he walked in, shook his head, then resumed collecting ammo, grenades, and a sidearm.

As usual, Richard was the last to step in. And as usual, as soon as he did, the energy seemed to evaporate out of the room.

Richard went with the standard plasma rifle, packing his vest with several additional magazines. He selected a Shipley-92 Semi-automatic plasma pistol with a seventeen-shot mag. Two grenades were slipped into his left pockets. Once he was done, he had sixty pounds of gear on him. It was an improvement over previous generations of marines. Battery magazines were far lighter than lead projectiles, and grenades nowadays were smaller, yet had a larger blast radius.

Most of the other soldiers carried the same weaponry, save for Foreman and Milla. Foreman held a Rico-97 Grenade Launcher in his arms. In its chambers were softball-sized explosives that, if shot into a machine gun nest, would send body parts flying for twenty yards. In addition, he had a vest full of demolition explosives.

"Better have them and not need them than need them and not have them," he said. He always said that. Once, the squad left an outpost to pick up a stranded pair of workers after their rover broke down. No threat, just a mechanical failure, and the team happened to be the closest to them. Sure enough, Foreman treated the assignment the same as if he was about to blow up an enemy bridge. He kept a shotgun on his back. "Just in case." Another phrase used before every drop.

"Good Christ…" Stevie muttered. He looked at Milla and the heavy machine gun she carried. "…Almighty!"

She winked and strutted past him, a submachine gun strapped over her shoulder. "I know how to handle big toys."

Portman cracked a smile and followed her out. "Is that right?"

"That is right," Foreman said. "Hence she's not interested in you, S.P."

More laughter at Portman's expense filled the armory.

"Alright, knock it off, ladies," Walker said. "Let's go. Move it out. Get your sorry asses to the bird." He looked down the hall toward the conference room. "Dante! Jerry! If you dipshits hold us up, I'm gonna be pissed."

"Coming!" Jerry said. There was a sound of a coffee mug being discarded and running feet coming toward the door. Jerry and Dante hustled down the hall toward the hangar. Both had their tool kits on hand, the heavier supplies already loaded on the dropship.

They followed the squad to the dropship.

The lighthearted banter was done and over with. Walker had allowed them to get it out of their system in the armory. Now, he expected his team to be all business. Even with the chance of a threat being low, he believed in planning for the worst.

The vertical shaft thrusters completed their rotation, the final checkup reaching its conclusion.

"Do I get the door gun, Sarge?" Milla asked.

"When we get down there, Tarasov," Walker replied.

"Yeah," Portman said. "Don't get too far ahead of yourself. You'll get us all sucked out into space."

"That'd be *mostly* tragic," Quinn said.

The rest of the marines and two engineers stepped aboard and fastened themselves to their seats.

Taking advantage of the extra space, Richard sat a couple of seats away from the others. Once they arrived on site, he would be able to form up on the exit ramp in no time. For now, he chose to keep his distance, something he figured the others preferred anyway.

He shut his eyes, wishing he was back in his cryo pod. Of all the planets he had to get yanked out of cryosleep for, it had to be the one Sara McQuade was on. Just another reminder of the misery that plagued his mind.

Just my dumb luck. Maybe God's rubbing it in.

The sound of someone taking the seat across from him made Richard open his eyes. It was Sergeant Walker. He clipped his restraints, then rested his hands on his battle rifle, his eyes fixed on the Corporal.

He leaned forward, keeping his voice low so the others wouldn't listen in. Not that it mattered. Everyone glanced in their direction every few seconds. Like school kids eagerly watching a fellow student get disciplined, they figured Walker was chewing Richard out.

Walker snapped his fingers in front of Richard's nose. The cracking sound was like a lightning bolt to Richard's brain.

"Snap out of it, Corporal," Walker said. "Not interested in your moping. Get your game face on."

Richard straightened his posture. "You still trust me?"

Walker's reply was simple. "Are you a marine?"

Richard nodded. "For now."

"Don't give me this 'for now' bullshit," Walker said. "Maybe Fort Matthews will put you on KP or make you a yeoman, but currently, you're still in my squad. So quit with the mental bellyaching."

Richard almost chuckled. Walker always had a phrase, 'assume I can hear the thoughts in your heads.' Strangely enough, it usually turned out to be true.

"Aye-aye, sir."

Walker leaned back, his hands resting on the barrel of his rifle. His eyes, surrounded by cracked, dry skin, were unblinking as they watched him. It was as though he was probing the Corporal's mind.

"You're thinking about your missus." It was a statement, not a question.

"Well... technically, she was never my missus," Richard said.

"Whenever someone has a relationship lasting longer than a night, it's practically a marriage these days," Walker said. "It's been six months. I'm not saying she's over it, but I think she's forgiven you."

Richard snorted. "You kidding, Sarge?" He tilted his head toward his fellow marines. "These guys haven't even forgiven me. Some have hardly spoken to me since."

"They'll live," Walker said.

"Live." Richard cracked a grin. It did not express joy, but bitterness. "At least they're alive."

"Three people are dead. Two researchers, one marine." Walker spoke in a matter-of-fact tone, as though he was completely disconnected from the situation. "Yes, it's your fault. Maybe they'll can your ass, maybe they'll keep you on. That's out of your hands for the most part. What happens in there..." he pointed to Richard's noggin, "...is in your hands. Get over it. Learn from it. Accept it. Move on."

Richard nodded. "Aye-aye, Sergeant."

The pilots made their announcement from the cockpit.

"Buckle in, keep all hands and feet in the vehicle at all times. We've got over seven hundred thousand kilometers to cross."

The warning light came on and the engines spun to life. Red flashers strobed throughout the hangar. Automated warning alerts twirled in the hangar, alerting all personnel to clear Hangar Bay Three.

"No, they're all still napping, ya dumb computer," Al said, letting his voice slip through the intercom.

The dropship's airlocks hissed shut.

The platform lowered and delivered the ship to its launch pad. There, the hangar bay door opened, revealing the deep vastness of space. In the middle of that infinite display of stars was a shiny blue planet.

Thrusters kicked on, launching the ship to its destination. Like a bullet discharged from a gun, it shot out of the side of the enormous freighter, quickly disappearing in the surrounding blackness. Only the blinking lights on the wings and the illumination coming through viewports made it visible to the naked eye.

Secondary thrusters kicked on, doubling the ship's speed. The ion engines went to work, guiding it past one of the planet's moons toward their mission.

Richard shut his eyes once more. Though he felt crummy, he tried to appreciate the relative simplicity of his misery. At least he had somewhat grown used to his colleagues hating him.

With Sara on board, the ride back would feel twice as long.
Lord, let this job be a simple pickup and dust-off...

CHAPTER 5

As they neared the planet Challenger, the details of its atmosphere and blue surface became distinct. The many islands scattered across the globe displayed their vibrant colors, some tropical, others mountainous. Like Earth, Challenger had polar ice caps on its north and south poles. It was spaced ninety-three million miles from its star, almost matching Earth's distance from the sun.

The viewing ports took on a fiery glow as the ship pierced the atmosphere. Turbulence juddered the passengers, each of whom glanced at the viewports. Though each of them were aware the outer shields were more than capable of handling the heat of atmospheric entry, there was still a feeling of unease.

The miniature crane and retrieval drone, secured by metal clamps, rocked in place. Jerry Morgalo, the head engineer assigned to the group, kept his eye on the device. He too, appeared to be rocking in place. His jaw was tense, his hands clutching the edge of his seat.

Both Richard and Walker watched him with great concern. Though the guy was former military, he did not appear to be handling this drop especially well.

"You better not lose your cookies," Sergeant Walker said.

"No, not that," Jerry said. He chuckled. "No risk of that. I'm just keeping the contents of my bladder from prematurely making an exit. I should've known better than to help myself to a hot mug of Joe before a drop."

Some of the marines laughed at his expense.

"Hope you get it all out of your system before we go back to cryosleep," Portman said.

"Depends on how many cups he snuck before we took off," Quinn said. "Ah, we'll be down there long enough for him to piss on the sand."

"Rocks, bozo," Milla said. "There're no sandy beaches where we're going. Just a big, boring atoll. Why they chose that place to do research is beyond me." She spoke with a fresh cigar tucked between her teeth. It was unlit, though that tragedy would be remedied the moment they touched down.

In the blink of an eye, the turbulence vanished. On the other side of the viewports were blue, sunny skies. Those who put their eyes to the reinforced glass saw clean, unpolluted ocean down below. It was a sight to behold. There was a purity to this water that nobody had seen in generations.

Before long, all the marines and engineers were staring out the viewports in awe of the new world below.

"Wow," Milla said. "So, this must be what pre-industrialized ocean looks like."

"Yep!" Quinn said. "Too bad it's been discovered. Give it about two more decades…"

Sergeant Walker detached his restraints and stood up. "Corporal, come with me to the cockpit."

Richard stood up and followed the Sergeant forward.

They opened the door to the cockpit and took in the view through the large, viewing panel. What they saw was infinite blue water with one little speck of light in the distance. Judging by the position of the sun, it was late morning in this region.

"See you've come to visit us, Sergeant," Al said.

"That our destination up there?" Walker said, his eyes locked on the island in the distance.

"As tempting as it was to check out that tropical paradise near the equator…" Al snickered, then quickly cleared his throat after realizing Walker did not share his sense of humor. "Yes, that's the island. Three miles out and closing. We've slowed to cruising velocity. Altitude, two thousand."

"Once we get there, decrease power to the main engines and engage the vertical rotors," Walker said. "Descend to eight hundred feet. I want to get a look at the island before we touch down." He turned to Richard. "Tell Milla she's good to go on manning the door gun."

Richard stepped into the fuselage, stopping and holding onto a safety handle in the bulkhead while the pilots slowly decreased altitude. Once they reached eight hundred feet, he turned to Milla.

"Tarasov, Sarge wants you on the gun. We're about to get our real-time overview of the place."

With the cigar still in her mouth, she gave an enthusiastic salute and went for the side door. After clipping on the safety tether, she slid the gunner's door open and stepped onto the platform. A rush of wind entered the dropship as she lowered herself onto the small exterior gunner's seat. Placing her hands on the butterfly grips, she panned the weapon side-to-side, praying for some kind of hostile threat to reveal itself.

Walker could be heard from the cockpit issuing orders to the pilots. "Ensign, initiate a radio call."

Roger Grill made the call. "This is Pelican-Four-Three-Eight, making a radio call to Smith Station. Smith Station, please respond... I repeat, this is Pelican-Four-Three-Eight calling Smith Station. Please respond... Hmm, not getting anything, Sergeant."

"Destination one thousand yards northwest," Al Jordan said. "Aaaand, we're here."

The southwest shore was now underneath the dropship. The pilots disengaged the aft thrusters and activated the vertical rotors, enabling the dropship to hover like an old-school helicopter.

Already, something seemed off with this island.

"Jesus," Milla said. "South shore's completely broken up. It does not match the original map."

"The Sergeant did say a section of the south side broke off," Richard said. "That's how they lost their vessel."

Milla leaned forward and looked at the water. "It's a steep drop-off. Not sure if we'll be able to recover their shuttle."

"Hell, looking at those rocks, I wouldn't be surprised if their shuttle is toast," Portman said.

Richard looked over his shoulder, seeing the infantryman attempting to look past him at the water.

"Portman, you mind?"

"Just trying to get a good view."

"There's windows for that," Richard said. "Get ready to form up on the ramp. All of you."

A few of the marines hesitated to follow the order, only doing so after their companions started taking position. They kept their lips zipped. Technically, his rank was still superior to theirs. Until that fact got corrected by Fort Matthews, they had to follow his lead.

As they formed up on the ramp, Sergeant Walker joined the Corporal and gunner at the starboard side door. The pilots initiated the patrol around the island, going east along what remained of the south shore.

"I see a personnel shack," Richard said.

"What's left of it," Walker said.

The vessel passed by the small living structure. Its entire front side had been torn open and broken into bits of debris. There was no sign of movement around it. Being several yards away from the jagged shoreline, it was unlikely the damage was done by seismic activity.

"Pirates?" Milla said. "Probably hit it with a high-charge energy blast."

"No," Richard said. "It'd be caved in. Looks more like it was torn out."

The ship reached the west shore and worked its way north. There was another shack a half-mile up. This one was in even worse condition. The entire structure had been torn down and reduced to a hundred pieces of scrap. Only the lack of energy burns eliminated the possibility of an explosion.

"Sweep the interior," Walker said to the pilots.

The craft moved inland, passing over rolling hills made of solid rock. There was not a single inch of vegetation or loose soil on this island. It was essentially a giant atoll, incapable of sustaining life, its own existence soon to reach its conclusion.

They reached the east shore, spotting the drone storage garage. Unlike the shacks, it was intact.

A few moments later, they arrived at the main facility.

"Oh, boy," Milla muttered.

The facility was in shambles. All four exterior walls were lined with impact craters and gashes. Pieces of steel had been torn out in ribbons, the front entrance reduced to scrap, the front lobby area a complete mess.

"Can't see any signs of blaster fire from up here," Richard said. "No movement either. We missed the party."

"What else could've done this?" Milla said, sweeping the landscape with the barrel of her machine gun.

"Not pirates," Walker said. "Wildlife, maybe."

"Never seen anything in the galaxy that could tear three-inch steel walls," Milla said. "Even the longtooth lions on

Storos would have a hard time, and their claws can rip body armor."

"It's a big galaxy," Richard said.

"Whatever it is, it was strong enough to bust the radio tower," Walker said. The other marines looked to the fallen structure northwest of the facility. The tower, which originally stood at twenty feet, had collapsed, the support legs on the west side crumpled like aluminum foil.

"One of the boats has taken a beating," Richard said. "Farthest one has damage to the bow section. Same kind of damage as the facility. Maintenance garage looks intact."

"What about that one?" Milla pointed out to sea, where a larger boat was anchored offshore. It was a Beluga-class gunship, refitted into a research vessel. The pilots took the dropship over the big boat. Its transom and wheelhouse had been splintered, the arm of its crane hung over the side.

There did not appear to be a single soul aboard. The pilots made an announcement over the speakerphone in case anyone was below deck. After a minute of trying, nobody came topside.

The Corporal took a breath, feeling his heart starting to thump wildly. The sight of the wreckage made his stomach tighten and his hands shiver.

Walker leaned toward him, obviously knowing his thoughts were on Sara McQuade. "Focus, Corporal. Keep your head in the game." After getting a nod from Richard, Walker turned his head toward the cockpit. "Ensign, any luck with the radio?"

"Negative, Sergeant," Roger replied. "We won't know if anyone's still alive unless we go down there."

"Well, we didn't come here for sightseeing," Walker said. "Find a spot to set down."

"I'll do my best, sir," Al Jordan said. "The problem is the south end of the island was the only level part of this rock. That's why they originally parked their own shuttle there. Even after the initial reported breakoff, there was still room to set down. Unfortunately, I think more of the island has broken away since."

"I think the island's lost some of its north end too," Roger added. "There originally was a peninsula beyond the radio tower. All I can say is there's nothing there anymore."

"There's probably less than a mile of this rock still intact," Walker said. "The scientists here weren't kidding when they spoke about seismic activity."

"The southwest shore between the two guard shacks was relatively smooth," Roger said. "We can try there."

"Don't have much of a choice," Al said. "Setting down anywhere else will wreck the landing struts."

Milla stepped back into the ship and unharnessed herself before joining the other marines at the ramp. Al steered the dropship southwest, finding a small stretch of rock near the water that was mostly level. He inched forward and side to side, trying to find a spot with as few bumps as possible. Almost everywhere he looked, the ship would be teetering unnaturally to one side or the other. After a few minutes of searching, he settled on a spot and committed. "Alright... setting down in three, two, one..."

Crunch!

Though the descent was slow and easy, the landing still felt as though the dropship had freefallen against the island. The ship teetered seven degrees to port, having landed on a slight incline.

The ramp came down.

The marines did not require an order. This was muscle memory, having been performed over a hundred times before.

In a heartbeat, they stormed the beach, guns at the ready. Even though they had not seen a soul during the flight sweep, they treated the area as though it was swarming with hostiles.

Within seconds, a perimeter was secured around the dropship.

"Corporal, check out the north wreckage and find any clues as to what occurred here," Walker said to Richard. "Foreman, Quinn, follow me to the south shack. The rest of you hold position here."

"No argument here," Jerry said. He remained inside the ship with Dante, the former's quirky demeanor having quickly shifted into stone-faced readiness. They had only been on this planet for a few minutes, and already this 'simple' job had gotten really interesting... and eerie.

"Jac, Stevie, on me," Richard said. He led his fireteam north while Walker's went south.

Everywhere the team looked, there was wreckage. Not one square foot of the shack was recognizable. The walls had been reduced to small pieces, some fragments crumpled and flayed as though put through some kind of chipper-shredder. The bed was destroyed, the mattress nothing but wet balls of foam. Clothing and personal items were scattered. Family photos were cracked, electrical tablets smashed against the rocks and wetted by rain. The only weapon found was a stun baton, used by private security and flight personnel. Whoever occupied this shack was probably the shuttle pilot, with nothing to do except hang around camp until the work here was complete.

As noted during the flight, there were no plasma burns of any kind. The shack had literally been ripped apart by brute force and sharp instruments.

"Got something here," Jac said.

Richard approached the infantryman, who was kneeled by the east wall. The rock and debris were stained with red, the ground littered with tiny strips of clothing and leather. Some of the bits were mashed up and covered in some kind of slimy substance. Currently, it was the brownish red staining that held the Corporal's attention.

"Blood?"

"Yep," Jac said. "At least a day old, in my estimation."

Richard stared at the blood and the debris around it. In the middle of the ruins, a tiny glass surface reflected the sun's glare. The Corporal knelt by the item and lifted it up.

"Got a badge here." He hit a small touchscreen button on the back. "Ted Hilden, shuttle pilot."

"Not anymore," Stevie said.

All three of them tensed as the ground seemingly came to life. The water began to thrash against the shore. There was an intense sound of cracking coming from *underneath* their feet, which had the three marines looking down.

"Everyone hold your position," Walker said through their radios.

A swift *crack* swept through the island, followed by the sound of splashing waves somewhere in the southern part of the island. Again, Walker's voice came through the radio.

"Fall back. We've got breakage."

At the dropship, Jerry and Dante voiced their astonishment as a huge chunk of the southwest shore broke away. Roughly four-hundred square feet of rock parted from the island, the seemingly smooth shore now free-falling into the water.

"Whoa! Holy shit!" Dante said.

The tremors gradually ceased, the waters calming after taking a bite out of the small stretch of land.

"Team Two, regroup at the dropship."

The order was followed before it was even issued. Richard, Jac, and Stevie double-timed it to the ship, the three of them feeling their throats tighten after seeing the alteration to the shoreline. The chunk of land had stopped short of the dropship by less than a hundred feet. The newly formed edge of the island looked more like a twenty-foot wall than a smooth shore. Broken fragments continued bouncing into the water, making tiny splashes as they joined the lost segment.

The pilots stepped outside, the alarm on their faces plain as day.

"A little too close for comfort," Al said.

"Not sure about you guys, but I'm not too keen on keeping this ship docked right here," Roger said.

Walker, Foreman, and Quinn arrived.

"Everyone all right?" the Sergeant asked.

"Won't be for much longer if we stay here," Al said.

"I concur," Walker said, his manner of speech much more formal than the co-pilot's. "Any luck on the radio?"

"Negative," Al said. "Nobody's answering."

"Their receiver's probably dead," Richard said. "If there are any survivors hiding in that facility, they probably don't even know we're here."

"Or... they ended up like that poor bastard at the shack," Stevie said.

"You located a body?" Walker asked.

"If you call splattered blood a body," Stevie said.

"One of the shuttle pilots," Richard clarified. "Deceased. Almost literally nothing left."

"Same over there," Walker said, tilting his head in the direction of the southernmost shack. "Co-pilot, Juan Santos. Found clothing, blood, and a severed foot still in the boot."

The engineers stepped back up the ramp.

"A severed foot?" Dante said. "Listen, boss, we've got two confirmed deaths. I think this might be the time for us to bug out and go home—before the planet gulps us down, or whatever did all this decides to revisit this place."

Walker gave his concern brief consideration, then shook his head.

"Pilots, have the ship ready for a quick departure if necessary. Engineers, don't bother with the equipment as of yet. I'm not worried about recovering the lost shuttle any longer. Marines, we're heading north to check out the rest of the island."

Dante threw his hands up. "Aw, come on, Sergeant! It's obvious nobody's left."

Jerry elbowed him hard in the ribs. "Shut up, ya coward. How'd you like it if we left *you* here to rot?"

Dante's face hardened, a few harsh comebacks rolling through his mind. He ultimately chose silence.

Walker looked to the pilots. "I want the two of you carrying weapons at all times. Keep your eyes peeled at all times. See or hear anything concerning, alert us through the radio."

"Way ahead of you, Sarge," Al said, slapping the plasma pistol holstered on his right hip.

Walker faced north and shouldered his rifle. "The rest of you, on me."

He took point, leading his squad to the main facility.

CHAPTER 6

The headache seemed as though it would never end. The tight quarters within the *Tortoise* were not intended to house its occupants for more than ten hours. It was going on seventy-two at this point, though those inside were just guessing at this point. Everything except life support had been shut off, conserving energy.

McQuade pressed her face to the viewing glass. The submersible was resting at a thirty-degree angle, its front side angled toward the surface. For twenty-four hours, they had been resting forty feet below the surface. Despite the efforts to preserve power, the *Tortoise's* energy core was running low.

"What's the matter?" John Kern said.

Sara kept her eyes to the glass, looking up at the glistening surface above. "Thought I had seen something."

"Saw what?" John asked. "Are *they* coming back?"

"No, something above the water," Sara said. "I think it may have been a ship."

"Just your imagination," Dr. Ben Cross said.

"No," Sara said. "I'm serious."

The station medical officer took a shallow breath. He was laying against the bulkhead, his natural color shifting into a sickly paleness. Lack of movement, water, and food were taking its toll. The place stank, for they all had to share the vac tube which was not getting backed up. The little air they had left was starting to dissipate.

"I'm sure you are," he said. "We've been trapped here for almost three days. We're dehydrated, tired, sensory deprived, emotionally wrecked, and scared shitless. We managed to escape while our friends were butchered, only to die here forty feet under the water."

Sara turned around, her nerves nearly at the point of snapping.

Seeing this, John put his hand on her shoulder. "Shh."

She pushed his hand away, her fiery eyes burning holes into the doctor. "Really, Ben? Is this the same Dr. Cross that performed an eleven-hour field surgery on a patient, while everyone else told you he wouldn't make it? The same Dr. Cross who preaches the importance of optimism?"

Ben removed a flask from his coat pocket and unscrewed the top. "That guy died long ago. Why else would I be on a measly explorer mission?" He took a swig. "I may have lost my 'sense of optimism' but I still have my common sense. There's no way out of here. We've got, at most, an hour of oxygen left. Even if someone did arrive, they have no way of knowing we're down here. Time to face the music, Sara. We're already in our coffin. The only optimism I can offer is the comfort that we won't be buried alone."

He took another swig.

Sara inhaled gently, then turned to rest against the glass. There was no sense in arguing with Ben. The guy had become a real negative Nancy in the last couple of years. However, logically speaking, she could not blame him in this instance. Even though they hardly moved since sinking, none of them experienced rest, especially not in the last twenty-four hours. The constant measuring of each breath to preserve air was taxing on the mind and body. On top of that, there was the lingering threat that lurked outside. The electrical ark flare was successfully able to repel the creatures, but that victory was hollow. The top hatch had been smashed, preventing them from making a desperate swim to the surface. The glass was bulletproof, as Dr. Cross had learned in the first hour after the sinking. The rudder and prop were heavily damaged in the attack, reducing the submersible into a five-million-dollar paperweight.

They were trapped here.

Sara turned her eyes toward the surface. If indeed she was going to die here, she would spend her remaining time watching the beautiful, sun-kissed water. Despite the horrors this ocean contained, there was still beauty to be seen. The surface, golden and bright, was the most beautiful part. It made her think of Heaven, which made the thought of death a little less scary. With that in mind, she kept her eyes pointed up.

Also, she still clung to the hope somebody had come…

***

It was a sight to behold.

Jac and Foreman took firing positions, providing cover for the rest of their squad as they advanced the remains of the facility. It was worse than how it looked from the dropship. The entire front of the building was unrecognizable. Pieces of insulation, exterior panels, support beams, glass, and other debris were torn open. At first glance, it almost appeared as though the front entrance had exploded from within.

Walker, Portman, and Milla held position in front of the breach, keeping their weapons pointed at the vast darkness within. Richard, Stevie, and Quinn were on their way back from inspecting the dock area.

As the Corporal had feared, it had been a bloodbath. He approached his Sergeant and shook his head.

"Just as bad as we feared," he said. "At least two fatalities over there. No bodies. Just bits of clothing, nametags, and tools. It was the station's engineering staff. My guess is they went to work on the boats, then got attacked by something."

"Found another fatality at the maintenance garage," Walker said. "Front door ripped out, pieces scattered everywhere." He turned his attention to the facility. "Carson, Jac, you two are with me. The rest of you, maintain the perimeter."

The three-man fireteam cautiously entered the building. Richard took point, igniting the flashlight under the barrel of his rifle. A white glow pierced the darkness, bringing to view the tattered floor panels and indented walls behind the main lounge.

He pressed inward, spotting a small hallway on the righthand side. At its end was the radio room. He aimed his light inside, finding the door open and the interior intact. Nobody was inside. The radio mic hung freely from its cord, as though abandoned suddenly.

Walker tested the lights. Nothing came on. The generators had likely stalled or run out of fuel.

"Personnel quarters in the next hallway," he said.

Richard emerged from the radio hall and led the team deeper into the facility. As they moved, their lights panned across the floor. There were odd piercings in the tile, as though someone had hammered camping stakes into the flooring and violently yanked them out.

They reached the next hallway, which led to the first set of crew quarters. Everyone had their own private bedroom, though they were very small, only containing a bunk and a laundry closet. The only electronic entertainment came from handheld tablet devices.

Richard performed a check of each room, pausing as he reached the end of the hall. At first glance, he thought the room at the end was twice as large as the others. Then he saw the pieces of wall scattered across the floor. The wall that divided the last two rooms had been completely cut down to size. The wall, made from metal sheets with insulation in-between them, now resembled wood chippings.

The bunk in the farthest room had been torn to shreds, the fabric and floor stained brownish-red. Something had torn through the place just to get at the poor soul who took refuge in here.

Richard aimed his light at the hallway floor. Like the main hall, it had been repeatedly pierced by multiple pointed objects. The spacing was narrower, suggesting that whatever did this was large and struggled to squeeze its way through this narrower hall.

Richard looked to Walker, held up one finger, then performed a slicing motion over his throat. *One individual. Deceased.*

The fireteam proceeded down the hall, finding a few more crew quarters. These ones were somewhat larger than the others, probably for the scientists. Each one was vacant, though it appeared that the drawers were hastily opened, as though the owners tried to retrieve important items during an evacuation.

At the end of this hall was a set of double doors, partially open. Walker pushed one with the barrel of his rifle, watching down the iron sights in case anything was waiting for them.

What they found was a large laboratory, which encompassed the back half of this building. Everywhere the marines looked, they saw high-tech equipment, ranging from simple microscopes to large cylinder-shaped machines whose function was beyond their understanding.

"What were they doing here?" Stevie asked. "Testing the water? Seems like an awfully big setup for something like that."

Walker wasn't concerned with that. What he was concerned with was the fact that nobody was in here. The lab tables in the middle of the room were overturned, their contents spilled across the floor. The back wall had been torn open in multiple places, leaving large chunks of jagged steel all over the place.

Richard saw shattered glass near the entry points, as if someone had thrown them at the intruders in a vain attempt to repel them.

"Last stand," Richard said. "They tried to hole up in here, but the threat managed to cut through the walls and crash through the doors."

"Shh!" Walker held up a fist, watching the back left corner of the room. Near the far end was a bend in the wall, which appeared to lead to an office or restroom.

In that little section of the lab was a scraping noise. An edged object was tapping against a piece of steel. There was the sound of bending metal and glass objects clattering against each other.

From where the marines stood, they could not get a visual. The anomaly was obscured by lab machinery, particularly a large rectangular object which stood at the corner of the wall. Past its edge, something lurked.

There was a wet, slimy sound, giving the men a mental image of a giant worm wiggling around that corner.

"The hell is that?" Stevie whispered.

Walker took the lead, slowly approaching the sound. He worked his way around a few overturned lab tables, making sure not to accidentally step on any glass or equipment along the way. They maintained complete silence, their rifle muzzles pointed at the northeast corner of the room.

Arriving near the big rectangular machine, Walker raised his hand to count down from three.

When the count hit zero, they turned the corner.

The thing raised its elongated head from the hole it had burrowed into the machine. Its disk-shaped body stood on four bony legs, with two additional forelegs rearing back like a praying mantis'. Its insectoid mandibles, comprised with a large pincer mouth surrounded by tiny digits, expanded. A deafening screech penetrated the air, making the marines step back.

Without hesitation, the creature darted in their direction.

Walker was the first to fire. His blaster bolt struck the creature in its chest area, severing one of its little arms.

A brief volley of energy projectiles finished the creature off, burning through its exoskeleton and incinerating the internal organs.

The strange insectoid-crustacean rolled on its back, its legs coiling under its body. After a few deathly twitches, the creature stiffened.

Walker, not one to take chances, put one more round in its head, reducing its brains to soot on the floor.

Foreman's voice echoed through the radio. *"We heard blaster fire. Everything all right in there, Sarge?"*

"Affirmative. Encountered some kind of…" Walker looked to a breach in the north wall. Somewhere outside, obscured by the intact sections of wall, a series of sharp tapping sounds approached the facility. "Stand by."

He, Richard, and Stevie readied themselves. Something was coming.

Emerging through the breach was another crustacean. It was slightly bigger than its deceased counterpart, its mandibles dripping with saliva. As soon as it laid eyes on the marines, it sprang to attack.

Walker squeezed off a shot. A blue strobe of energy struck the creature between the eyes and split its head open.

As soon as its corpse hit the floor, three more arrived at the breach. Hungry creatures with no consideration for the weapons their prey possessed, they darted into the lab.

Richard pulled off a shot, stopping one of them in its tracks. The target reeled backward, its legs kicking madly while a greenish blood spurted from its carapace.

Stevie and Walker neutralized the other two.

"Whoa! Holy hot damn!" Stevie exclaimed as he put a dozen shots into his target. The creature's corpse expanded, the innards sizzling from the heat of his projectiles.

Walker handled the last one with efficiency, putting two shots in its torso and one in its head. He moved to the breach and swept the outside perimeter with the muzzle of his rifle. There were a few other of these creatures scurrying near the shore, seemingly unaware of their companions' fates.

Not one to take chances, Walker fired several rounds, killing one of them and driving the others back into the water.

"The team's ready, Sarge," Foreman said.

"Copy that. Stand by," Walker said. He continued watching the shoreline for any more of these things. "All clear. All units, watch your surroundings. We ran into some local wildlife. Don't know what to call them. They're crustacean in appearance, with insect qualities. They're highly aggressive, so watch your backs."

"Copy that," Foreman said. *"What are your orders, sir?"*

"Maintain position. We have not located any survivors. It appears that all personnel are deceased. Have Jac get a log of our findings. Get snapshots of the damage so we have something to report back to headquarters."

"Roger that."

Stevie stood over one of the dead creatures. "Ugly little bastards." He prodded its mandibles with his rifle. "I imagine it latches onto you and chews you up. Kinda like how a praying mantis eats. Mantis, mantid... screw it. Sea-mantid."

"Sounds about right," Richard said.

"Hate to be the poor bastard who goes out like that." Stevie shuddered from the thought.

"Let's finish the job before more of them show up." Walker looked at the surrounding damage. "Or something worse."

Stevie looked at the large rectangular machine that it had dug into. He couldn't help but chuckle when he realized what it was. Reaching at the small handle in its corner, he opened the door to a refrigerator unit.

"Thought it was highly advanced lab equipment," he said. "Well, I guess scientists need a cold one after a long day of work." He reached in and snatched a beer from the back of the fridge. "Damn. Stallion-Nova! They have the good stuff here. Our little buddy was probably trying to go for some of the cold cuts on the bottom shelf." He bumped the first dead crustacean with his boot.

Richard felt his blood rushing. A sense of hopelessness descended on him like a swarm of locusts. The sight of the carnage, wreckage, and the razor-sharp mandibles possessed by the crustaceans painted a terrible picture of Sara McQuade's fate.

"Sarge?"

"You alright, Corporal?" Walker asked.

Richard ignored the question. "We should keep looking. Maybe the survivors are elsewhere..."

"There is no 'elsewhere'," Walker said. "This is it. The boats are damaged and vacant. The lab is wrecked. The drone station is unattended. I'm sorry, Corporal, but she's dead. Whatever happened here, we missed it. If I knew they were alive somewhere, I'd stay. But for now, we need to catalogue our findings and vacate before the rest of this island crumbles." The Sergeant placed a comforting hand on Richard's shoulder, then moved into the hallway. Before exiting, he stopped and pointed a finger at Stevie. "Marine, if you drink that while on duty, rest assured, I'll see to it you remain awake for the rest of the trip home. No cryosleep for you."

Stevie dropped the beer and smiled. "You're the boss, Boss."

They exited the lab, leaving Richard standing defeated. He felt as though he had awoken from a deep sleep only to enter a real-life nightmare. For the last six months, he tried to forget about Sara as heavily as he tried to forget about his failure. She had partially relocated to this planet because of his mistake. And because of that mistake, she was now dead.

Richard stepped through one of the breaches in the north wall. A wave of salty air swept over him. Finding a patch of elevation, he watched the water. Sara had once said something about the waves having a calming effect on her.

Unfortunately, it was not having the same effect on him. Especially with that boat adrift way out to the east. There wasn't anyone on it. They had flown over it during their initial pass and attempted to call with the megaphone. Nobody tried to flag them down.

He remembered the state of the deck and wheelhouse. Whoever was on that boat likely met the same fate as the people in the lab.

"You okay?"

Hearing the familiar Russian accent, Richard turned around as Milla stepped through the north wall.

"Yeah. Just admiring the view," he said.

She walked up the rock mound and stood beside him, watching the blue water sweep ashore.

"It is a pretty view," she said. "Too bad it holds some deadly secrets."

"Sarge have you cataloging?"

Milla held up her small camera. "Would rather be shooting plasma bolts instead of pictures. Looks like you guys got to experience the only fun to be had on this rock." She pointed her thumb over her shoulder in the direction of the dead crustacean. "You think that's what did all of this?"

Richard scoffed. "I highly doubt it." He focused on that boat adrift to the east. His eyes shifted between that and the boats on the dock. One appeared to be undamaged and fully functional.

A grain of hope took form in his mind.

"Oh, no," Milla said. "I know what's going on in that brain of yours. Forget it, Corporal. Your woman is dead. I'm sorry."

"Sarge said we need to catalogue everything."

"Yeah…"

"So, we'll need to get images of that boat. Come on." Richard jogged to the docks. Milla groaned, then followed him.

"Corporal, stop doing this to yourself."

"Let me get this out of my system, will ya?"

He climbed aboard the vessel and gave a brief glance at its deck. A small tool kit and an electronic monitor were placed near the transom. Behind the cockpit deck was a drone, similar to the ones beached on the east shore. It was probably a boat used for conducting underwater research with the use of the drones. Perhaps they were making scans of the seabed and collecting samples. Richard wasn't sure—he was no scientist. Nor did he really care—there were more pressing issues to focus on.

He took a seat at the cockpit and started the engine. Straight ahead, Sergeant Walker approached from the front of the main building.

"Corporal? What are you doing?"

"Getting images of the boat out there," he said. "Right, Milla?"

She groaned again, then climbed aboard. "Certainly."

Walker nodded. He knew the real reason why Richard was going out on the water, but he was letting it go. The need to catalogue the findings was technically true, after all.

"Keep your eyes peeled," the Sergeant said. "We still don't know what caused all of this. Whatever it was, it was better than that sea-mantid thing in the lab."

"Aye-aye, sir."

Milla detached the mooring lines and took position on the starboard aft section of the boat. "Good to go, Corporal." Her eyes were on the water, looking out in case any nasty secrets chose to reveal themselves.

Richard reversed the boat away from the dock, turned it around, and pointed its bow at the derelict boat. There was a moment of hesitation. His mind screamed warning about the true likelihood of finding Sara. Slim to none. If she was on that boat, the reality of the situation was, at best, that he would find her remains. He wasn't sure if he was mentally prepared for that. On the other hand, if he left a single stone unturned, he would never be able to sleep at night.

He pushed the throttle and sped the boat to its destination.

***

Sara felt her eyes drooping. Each breath felt empty, making her wonder if there was even less oxygen than they previously thought. Dr. Ben Cross was lying flat on his back, flask at his lips. He was half-asleep, having accepted his fate. Sara couldn't blame him. In a sense, it was better than the horrible deaths their colleagues suffered.

"You okay?" John Kern asked. He was lying on his side, resting his head on his arm. Almost all of his energy had evaporated, rendering his speech slurred. His eyes were shut for several moments at a time. Like Ben, it seemed he was done fighting and ready to accept his fate. Even in this moment, he felt the need to check up on his colleague.

Sara chuckled weakly. "Yes. Considering we're gonna be dead shortly."

"I see you're still looking out the window."

"The water is nice. The sun's out. Puts me at ease." She turned her eyes back to the water's surface. The sun's rays sparkled as they pierced the water. It was a soothing view. While she wished to live on, she chose to concentrate on the positive. There were worse ways to go than drifting off after watching the sunlight sparkling under the water's surface. Everything was tranquil, gentle, and undisturbed... until it wasn't.

Even with her hazy vision, the sight of the vessel cutting across the water was unmistakable. Like an aircraft coming in for a landing, it reduced speed as it neared its destination.

New energy filled Sara's body. She stood on her knees, eyes wide, a smile coming over her face. The sight of the space vessel was not a figment of her imagination. Someone had come to rescue them. Common sense suggested the rescue team had found the remains of their settlement and were now inspecting the boat.

"You see something?" John asked.

"Someone's here," she replied.

John hurried over to the glass and looked up. "Oh, praise the Lord."

A pessimistic laugh from Ben Cross immediately killed their newfound optimism. He took another drink from his flask and shook his head, booze dripping from his lips.

"Oh, yay. Great. Too bad we're all the way down here," he said. "Not like they have any way of knowing we're down here."

There was no point in wasting time arguing with him. John went for the radio station, clicking a few switches in a vain attempt to get a signal out.

"If they're this close, maybe they can pick up a transmission," he said.

"Won't happen," Ben said. "The transmitter got crushed in the attack. On top of that, Sara used up most of our remaining power to repel the things with an electrical charge."

"You sound bitter," Sara said.

Ben shrugged. "Well, if we had just accepted our fate instead of driving them off, the worst would already be over and you wouldn't have the false hope of rescue."

"Ben, just... be quiet please," John said. He fumbled with the controls, trying desperately to come up with a clever solution. He desperately engaged the throttle, knowing full well that the prop was smashed. "Damn it." He put his eyes to the glass. The boat had pulled up alongside the other, the newcomers likely searching for survivors. "Maybe they'll look down and see us."

Ben snorted. "We're over forty feet down, John. You seriously think they'll just glance at the water and go 'Oh! Hey look! There's a submarine down there!'?" He crossed his feet and shut his eyes. "Unless something somehow manages to draw their attention to this sub, we're screwed. Not like we have a functioning spotlight to flash at them."

That statement ignited a thought in Sara's brain.

"No... not a spotlight." She went to the main controls.

"Mind sharing what your big idea is?" John asked.

"Getting their attention," she said. She flipped a few switches on the overhead panel, directing power from the core to the outer shell. At that point, John understood the plan.

"An ark flash... yeah, they should see that," he said. "I just hope their eyes will be on the water when it happens. The charge won't last long. You only have enough power for one or two quick flashes."

"Yeah..." Sara hit a few buttons on the main panel. A small screen lit up with red LED letters: *Air release ready.* Sara gave the computer a chance to siphon the air and direct it to the expulsion system. "Gonna let some air out. Hopefully that'll make them look at the water in time for the flash."

John opened his mouth to protest. His first inclination was to point out that if this plan failed, it would leave them with five minutes of oxygen at most. He then remembered that suffocation was guaranteed one way or another at this point. This was their only chance for survival.

He nodded.

Sara counted down from three, then pulled the lever. Watching the air bubbles rise to the surface, she placed her hand on the overhead switch. In thirty seconds, she would trigger the ark flash. As she counted down, she prayed for her plan to work.

***

The inspection of the vessel only took a few short moments. There wasn't much to check. There was a small cargo hold under the main deck, which was empty. The hull had suffered numerous lacerations, and the deck was smothered in somebody's blood. It was dry and discolored now.

Milla snapped images of the control console—what was left of it. The helm was broken into several pieces and the top panel had been slashed by something huge and incredibly sharp. Like the station's hallways, the deck had been punctured by multiple sharp objects.

The heavy gunner shook her head and looked at Richard. "Sorry, Corporal. We both knew there was little chance anyone would be aboard."

Richard held his hand toward her, successfully shutting her up. Sighing heavily, he crossed back over to the functional vessel.

"Come on," he said. "Nothing more we can do. Let's just get the hell out of here."

Milla stood at the center of the deck, looking at the large crane that hung over the portside. A cable swayed from its arm, its frayed tip grazing the water's surface.

"What do you think they used this for?"

"Who cares?" Richard said. "It doesn't matter. Everyone's dead. There's nothing we can—" He perked up, his ears picking up a strange *popping* sound. He looked to the water, seeing air bubbles bursting several meters off the starboard bow.

"The hell's that?" Milla said.

"Air bubbles," he said.

"No... *that!*" She pointed a finger at the water. "There it is again."

This time, Richard saw it too. It was an electrical flash of some kind coming from the seabed. Whatever it was, it originated from the exact same point as the air bubbles.

The air bubbles and flashing stopped simultaneously, the ocean returning to its calm and silent state.

Richard squinted, trying desperately to see what was causing the flash.

"Should we alert the Sarge?" Milla asked.

"Not yet." Richard turned around and walked to the drone unit. "Is this linked to this little monitoring device?"

Milla knelt down next to it. "Yeah. Looks like it still has power. Shouldn't be hard to operate. Use the joystick to turn left, right and so forth."

Realizing what his plan was, she linked the drone to the tablet device, then helped the Corporal lower it into the water. The screen on the tablet came to life, displaying the side of their own boat.

Richard pressed his thumb to the joystick and submerged the drone. Down it went, descending dozens of feet. Its camera pointed at the seabed. With the exception of some seaweed and other vegetation, it was almost as rocky as the island that was splitting apart. It was shallower than he expected, considering the fact that the island was sinking.

As he turned the device west, he understood why. There was a drop-off between this area and the island. In that moment, an aftershock rippled through the crust, knocking a few loose pebbles into the widening crevice.

It served as a reminder that he needed to act fast.

Richard turned the drone east and aimed it toward the area where they saw the flash.

His heart fluttered. In the middle of that rocky seabed was a yellow lump comprised of reinforced steel.

An exploratory submersible.

"Holy shit," Milla exclaimed.

Richard steered the drone closer, zooming its camera on the sub's cockpit. On the other side of the glass was a woman in her early thirties. Her hair was dark, her skin golden-brown, her eyes—though he couldn't see them in this moment—as blue as the water itself.

She put both hands on the glass, then smiled as she spotted the drone.

Richard smiled. "Found you."

The woman's upbeat demeanor started to shift into one of panic and dread. She was hunched over, rocking back and forth, her mouth hung open.

"Something's wrong," Milla said. "It almost looks like she's struggling to breathe."

"Oh, no." He brought the drone closer, getting a view of two men who were trapped in the sub behind her. They were conscious. Barely. The Corporal quickly connected the dots. "They're almost out of oxygen. We need to get them up."

"How the hell are we gonna do that?" Milla said.

Richard looked at the Beluga-class hauler. With the cable busted and the controls disabled, there was no way they could use it to lift the sub on deck.

That left the standard vessel on which he and Milla stood aboard. He gave a quick look to the main deck. Though smaller in comparison to the other vessel, it still granted enough space for what Richard had in mind.

He lifted his radio to his lips. "Sergeant!"

"Go ahead, Corporal."

"Looks like we're gonna need that crane after all."

CHAPTER 7

It was twelve feet in length. Its jaws were lined with hooked teeth, designed for snagging the hides of large whales. Rigid scales formed a suit of armor around its flesh, protecting it against most other predators that dwelled in the shallow ocean waters of Challenger.

Unbeknownst to the creature, its species had been given the name Sickle-Tooth by the human visitors. Its teeth were razor sharp, not only capable of piercing the flesh of larger creatures, but also very effective at prying loose the armored scales from other sickle-tooth fish. Only the hawk eel rivaled its aggression.

In recent days, it had encountered an adult of equal length. Though the hawk eels did not have the thick body mass of the sickle-tooth, they had superior agility. The encounter did not go well for the sickle-tooth, with the eel using its snake-like body to constrict its opponent, holding it in place while the beak cracked through the armor plates.

The sickle-tooth had escaped the encounter with its life and only minor damage. Since then, it swam around its normal hunting grounds on the west side of the island in hopes of finding weak or injured prey. Much of the natural wildlife near the island had been driven out since the deep dwellers moved in. Hordes of coral squid, which congregated in little hives within the rock, had been driven out or slaughtered. The invertebrates had been picked clean from the surrounding burrows. This not only robbed the sickle-tooth of easy prey, but also stopped the inflow of larger fish and seals to the area, which it would have also gorged on.

It was late morning now. Having gone without food for two days, the sickle-tooth had ventured into the open ocean. For miles, all it found were schools of measly insectoid-shrimp which, unbeknownst to it, had been coined as sea-mantids by the humans above. Small and agile, the crustaceans evaded its large jaws. Four feet in body length, they were aggressive to other species of similar size, but scattered in the presence of a larger creature. Only if said predator was severely injured were the mantids brave enough to engage in combat.

Finding nothing of substance, the sickle-tooth returned to its normal feeding grounds. It avoided the south side of the island. At this point, it did not have the energy for another violent encounter with the hawk eel. The fish needed an easy meal, and soon. Its twelve-foot mass required a lot of energy just to move. Maintaining a gradual pace, it patrolled the east and north sides of the island, letting the water run through its nostrils.

Finally, it picked up the scent of blood. Blood in the water meant dead or injured prey was nearby. The source, whatever it was, was somewhere in the shallows.

The sickle-tooth swam to investigate, swinging its large fan-shaped caudal fin back and forth. It came across a steep slope that acted as the stem of the island. The world around it had been splitting apart due to the violent shaking. All around it were deep crevices where the crust had split.

It swam over the deep abyss and approached the mountainous incline. This area was less steep than other sections of the seabed, still maintaining remnants of the ecosystem that once dwelled here.

As the fish ascended, the smell of blood intensified. It found the source less than fifty feet from the shore. Laying against the rocks was another sickle-tooth. It was a juvenile, only having grown to eight feet. Its tail was gone and its hide was flayed open, exposing the rib bones and spine. Much of the meat had already been picked clean, with only some remaining near the head and gills.

Scattered around it were the remains of mantids.

Legs, forelegs, and pieces of shell had been discarded for dozens of yards.

The fish did not have the brain capacity to contemplate the cause of the massacre. In every animal kingdom across the universe, predators slaughtered prey and scavengers took what was left. Though the sickle-tooth had never seen such vast quantities of dead mantids, it passed over their remains without concern. It did not sense any movement in the area. Only large rocks.

It closed in on the dead fish and nudged the gill area. There wasn't much meat left, but a small meal was better than nothing at all. It parted its jaws and bit at the remains.

Sensory receptors in its snout picked up tiny electrical discharges—the kind caused by movement. It paddled its pectoral fins and turned to its left.

The 'rocks' that were huddled near the dead fish stood up on long, prickly legs. Arms unfolded, their serrated ends yawning open like the jaws of an eel. In this moment, the fish realized it had wandered into a trap. The crustaceans, who usually lurked in the deeper regions of the ocean, had sprung a trap.

In the blink of an eye, the fish found itself snared by their sharp claws. The pincers shut with intense force, their razor-sharp edges cutting through the armor scales with ease.

The next smell of blood was its own.

Though smaller in size, the creatures demonstrated superior strength. The sickle-tooth's efforts to swim away resulted in it swimming in place. One of the creatures pinched down on its left pectoral fin and its underbelly, its legs dug firmly into the seabed to prevent it from being lifted out.

With escape no longer an option, the fish opted for a new course of action: attack. It angled its jaws toward one of the rear legs and bit down with tremendous force.

Crack!

Pain surged through its entire mouth as multiple teeth splintered. The shell covering the crustacean's limb hardly displayed a scratch. The beast was literally impenetrable.

Unable to pull itself free, the sickle-tooth bit again, only to suffer the same result. Blood now billowed from its mouth as well as its fin and belly.

Its companion scurried behind the fish and secured a grip on its tail. Utilizing their combined strength, they wrestled the large fish onto its side. Pinned against the rocks, the sickle-tooth could do nothing except squirm as its body was flayed open.

Its slayers, void of empathy or compassion, did not care that their actions caused intense pain and suffering. In fact, the struggles of their victims only spurred them to act more cruelly. It was a display of dominance, for they were the dominant species on the planet, feared by even the largest of whales and fish. That need to display dominance rivaled their need to feed.

The creatures paused, holding the dying fish in place as they detected new vibrations. These were not coming from the planet's crust, but in fact isolated segments of the island. New lifeforms were present—lifeforms that solely lived above the water.

Both creatures simultaneously experienced the memory of slaying the other bipedal inhabitants of the island. The taste of their flesh was tender and juicy, vastly superior to the tough meat of the fish, whales, and other species they were used to. For the first time, the crustaceans experienced true pleasure in the simple act of eating. They learned the joy of *taste*.

Nothing tasted better than humans.

Their only concern was beating their brethren to the food. There was one other need to satisfy first.

They resumed torturing their current victim, who squirmed as large chunks of flesh were torn from its body. Once the deed was done, the crustaceans would take their pincers to the soft meat on shore.

CHAPTER 8

"Holy shit. The hell's going on out there?" Roger Grill said. The co-pilot stood by the dropship's ramp, cupping his hand over his eyes as he watched the strange thrashing in the water. Fifty feet out, there appeared to be some kind of struggle taking place.

"Whoa!" Al Jordan said. He stepped out of the cockpit and beheld the sight of blood clouding around the disturbance.

"The hell is that?!" Roger said.

Al shrugged. "My best guess? Nature's taking its course out there."

Roger's hand instinctively rested over his sidearm. He backed into the dropship and watched from one of the viewing ports. He could not see what was struggling, nor was he eager to know. After hearing the reports of the squad's findings on this island, all Roger cared about was getting out of here as quickly as possible.

For better or worse, their stay was prolonged. To everybody's amazement, Corporal Carson and Milla Tarasov located survivors stranded underwater, of all places. Before departing with the crane and drone, Jerry speculated the research group had a submersible for exploratory purposes. For whatever reason, the seacraft was disabled. The engineers had to act fast to get the crane across the island and aboard the one functioning boat.

Ultimately, he was glad. If the submersible was disabled, the people inside were doomed to suffocate eventually. Thanks to Richard and Milla's attention to detail, this mission resulted in lives being saved. The marines and engineers were currently working to get them out of the water.

For now, all the pilots could do was wait.

Roger watched the water. The violent thrashing drew to an end, the circle of life now completed for the loser in this encounter. Blood, guts, and rigid, disc-shaped remains rode the bloody surf to the shoreline. Curious, he stepped outside for a better view.

Those things almost looked like fish scales. *Big* fish scales.

Hate to see the fish those belonged to. His eyes went to the spot where the thrashing took place. *And I'd REALLY hate to see whatever just killed it.*

Al Jordan was thinking the same thing. The two pilots shared a nervous glance.

"Hope those guys hurry up over there," Al said.

***

By the time Jerry and Dante arrived with their equipment, Richard had the boat backed up against the shoreline. The vessel, also designed for carrying heavy equipment such as the submersible, had a stern ramp which dropped at the pull of a lever. As soon as the ramp hit the shore, Jerry drove the crane aboard. Dante walked behind the vehicle, carrying the maintenance drone. Originally intended to attach the cable to the colony's shuttle, it was now going to attach it to the sunken submarine.

Quinn followed the engineers aboard. Heeding the Corporal's warning, he brought some respiratory equipment with him.

"We need to hurry," the medic said. "If they used oxygen to alert you, that means they probably don't have much left."

As soon as they were aboard, Richard raised the ramp and gunned the engine. During those few moments, Dante anchored the crane onto the deck and Jerry extended the arm.

"We sure we don't want to use the lift bags?" Dante said.

Jerry glanced at the underwater airlift bags they had in the crane's aft storage unit. "No. We're gonna need to attach the cable anyway and lift the sub onto the boat. It'll be faster this way."

"You're the boss," Dante said.

Richard stopped the boat near the sub's location and dropped the anchor. As soon as they stopped, Dante deployed the drone. It splashed down with the cable in tow. Using a portable control panel, Dante increased its depth.

A vast area of seabed filled the screen. The engineer turned the drone to and fro in search of the sub.

"Where is it—hey!"

Richard snatched it out of his hand and directed the drone toward the sub. With no time to waste, he centered the target on the screen and closed the distance before giving the device back to Dante.

The engineer accepted it with a not-so-subtle hint of bitterness. A few remarks came to mind, but he kept them to himself. He landed the spider-shaped drone on top of the sub, locating a few steel loops where the original cable had been clamped.

He attached the cable and gave a thumbs up to Jerry.

"Bring 'em up."

Jerry retracted the cable. There was a mild shift in the boat as the submersible was lifted off the bottom.

Quinn and Milla stood at the console with Richard, eagerly awaiting the arrival of the survivors. Seconds seemed like hours, each one longer than the last.

With an enormous splash, the submersible rose from the ocean. Jerry swung it over the guardrail and planted it on the deck.

Immediately, the crew noticed the intense damage to its hull. The rudder and propeller appeared as though someone had taken a giant can opener to them. In numerous places, the hull was indented. Several thick abrasions lined the sides and the fins. One of the arms had been ripped away entirely, the other crushed in multiple points. Even the glass showed signs of damage, with heavy scratches from something large and sharp.

"Dang," Dante said. "This is Landoran steel. What the hell could do this kind of damage?"

Richard and Quinn climbed to the hatch. They turned the wheel to unlatch it, but the door was jammed shut. The metal around the edges was folded over the hatch, as though a giant hammer and sickle had pounded into the machine.

"Hang on, let me see," Jerry said. The marines climbed down to make room for him. He climbed atop the sub and inspected the hatch. "Oh, hell. I can weld through this, but it'll take several minutes."

Richard put his face to the glass. The three people inside were unconscious, their mouths open as though their last seconds were spent gasping for breath.

"They don't have a few minutes." He stepped back and pointed his rifle at the upper frame of the glass. Jerry hopped off the sub and joined his staff member near the crane.

Richard squeezed the trigger. Multiple plasma bolts struck the reinforced glass. It took three shots to crack it and three more to breach. Scalding hot shards fell to the deck. With the rest of the glass weakened, Richard, with the aid of Quinn, smashed the rest of the visor.

The three people inside, Sara McQuade and two men, lay motionless.

The medic knelt by the nearest male, brushing some of the loose shards away from his head. He checked his vitals, then performed some chest compressions.

Richard knelt by Sara's side and did the same. He placed two breaths, then performed ten compressions. On the tenth one, Sara McQuade returned to life with a deep gasp. She sat up, hands on her chest, her mouth and eyes wide, as though awoken from a horrible nightmare.

"Sara! Sara!" Richard grabbed her shoulders. "We're a rescue team. We're here to help."

Sara took several breaths, her mind slowly grasping her new reality. The last thing she remembered, she was sucking the air for any last remaining molecules of oxygen before passing out.

Richard put a hand on her shoulder to keep her calm. Having been oxygen deprived, she was in a hazy state, not quite sure where she was at.

Her two companions were in a similar state. They awoke slowly, both groggy and unsure of where they were.

The one in the back, who held a flask in his hand, was the first to speak. "What the—what's going on?"

"Hang tight, sir," Quinn said. He looked at the Corporal and grinned. "They'll be alright. They just need a few minutes for their brains to fire back up."

Richard nodded. He lifted his hand from Sara's shoulder. To his surprise, she snatched it back and held it close to her chest. Though her eyes were closed, it was as though she sensed something familiar about the touch of his hand.

"You'll be okay, Sara... Dr. McQuade," he said.

She looked to her savior. For a second time, she gasped.

"R-Rich?"

The Corporal nodded. "Yeah, it's me." His stomach felt as if it was being squeezed by an invisible hand. Memories of past events haunted his mind. For the briefest of moments, he swallowed his feelings and put on a hardened shell of professionalism.

Like a ghost tormenting his soul, his mind flashed to the memory of a man in his upper thirties, finely dressed in field gear, rimmed glasses, and a short buzz cut worthy of the military.

Martin.

The memory played like a home video. In it, the man and Richard traded verbal jabs, drawing laughter from nearby people. Sara McQuade interjected herself into the banter session.

"Alright, knock off the beer pong, you dummies. Martin, if you keep acting like a first-year college student, I might have to change my last name to something else. Because when people hear the name Dr. McQuade, they might confuse the intelligent one, ME, with the goofball geologist getting wasted at fifteen hundred with the marines."

"Change your name, huh?" The ghostly figure named Martin looked at Richard and grinned. *"I think she's making hints, buddy. Ball's in your corner."*

Laughter followed.

The image vanished behind a wall of blinding light. When it faded, Richard was staring into a rocky landscape, covered in thick smoke and the wreckage of heavy industrial equipment. Scattered throughout the area were human corpses. Some were violent insurgents, each of whom carried some kind of weapon. Then there were the innocents.

One in particular stood out above the rest.

A man with a short haircut, dressed in field gear, lay on his back. Cracked glasses had fallen several feet away, never to be worn again.

"Corporal? Corporal?... Richard?!"

He looked up, the sound of Milla's voice snapping him back to reality.

"Let's go," she said.

"Right." He tried to pull his hand away from Sara so he could return to the console. She held on tight, as though her life depended on it. A deep uneasiness came over her.

Finally, she looked into Richard's eyes. Any awkwardness and concern for their history had been cast aside, for something more dire was at play. She winced, her entire head seized by a sharp migraine. Scattered memories began to return. Individually, they had no context. Together, they had one horrible meaning. Spurred by this revelation, she managed one statement.

"We all need to get out of here. *Now.*"

***

"Oh hell." Roger Grill tensed, clutching one of the seats to retain balance. This tremor was a violent one. The ocean grew angry, throwing eight-foot cresting waves against the shoreline.

A deep *crunch* echoed from the southern shore.

Roger heard his commanding officer yell from outside. "Get inside, Roger!"

In that moment, Roger saw a wall of water extend vertically from the south shore. A section of landmass had broken away and joined the underwater landscape.

The shakes proceeded, causing further damage. Waves crashed into the newly formed cove on the southwest shoreline. Small fragments of land broke away and fell into the water, gradually shortening the hundred-foot stretch of land which separated the dropship and the ocean.

Slowly, the earthquake began to settle down. Roger released his grip on the seat and exhaled slowly. For a moment, he thought he would have to retreat into the cockpit and make an emergency liftoff.

For the next few moments, he kept a sharp eye on the south shore. Though the tremors had stopped for the moment, Roger was still fearful that more of the island would break away.

A cold wind entered the ship, making the co-pilot shiver. He could not believe that an hour ago, he was contemplating owning a beach house on this planet. The majestic oceans and clean air had an intoxicating effect.

Now he could not wait to leave this place and never look back.

He listened to the crashing waves.

"Whoa! Geez!" Al exclaimed.

Roger peeked outside, seeing the huge wall of water break apart on the west shore. The mist swept for dozens of yards before raining down in small droplets. Al was fifteen feet from the port bow, wiping the salty water from his face.

After several impacts, the ocean began to settle down.

"You okay there, boss?" Roger said.

Al's face strained as he wiped his sleeve over his eyes. "Damn, that stings like a bitch. That water's really salty."

"That's what you get for watching the feeding frenzy," Roger said. An aftershock wiped his grin off his face. Watching the ground, wondering if it would split apart beneath his feet, he backed up the ramp.

It was a minor tremor which only lasted a few seconds. Roger took a seat, keeping his eyes focused on the fragile southern edge of the island.

He heard another splash of water from outside, followed by a shriek from Al Jordan.

"Whoa! BLECH!!!"

His complaints came to an abrupt end.

Roger chuckled. "Let me guess, you got splashed again. Ya dumb ass." He waited for a response, which never came.

A burst of static from the comms made him jump. Milla Tarasov's voice came through the receiver. Her voice was a welcome one, as was the news it brought.

"We got 'em," she said. *"They're alive and conscious."*

"Well done," Sergeant Walker responded. *"Any injuries?"*

"Nothing too severe," she replied.

"Get back to shore. We just had another quake. Flight crew, you guys all right over there?"

Roger took a seat. He assumed Al would answer the call, for he tended to do most of the talking. Oddly, the Command Pilot was silent. Roger couldn't even hear his pained groans. Just a strange, wet, peeling sound coming from outside.

The co-pilot lifted his head. That wet sound was not from the surf. It almost made him think of the messy process of shredding a greasy chicken. In addition, there was a strange pricking sound, as though someone was tapping a branch across the rocks.

"Pilot crew?" Walker continued. *"Answer me."*

Roger swallowed. There was no mistaking the next sound. He knew what fabric sounded like when it was being ripped.

He got on his feet, hurried down the ramp, and looked in Al's direction.

All of a sudden, the earthquakes were the last thing on Roger Grill's mind. He stood in stunned silence, seeing Al Jordan's dismembered body on the ground. His head was severed, his face pointed directly at Roger. His final gaze expressed the very pain he endured when his neckbone snapped.

Standing over him was an eight-legged creature. Blue in color, it resembled a giant arachnid at first glance. Then he saw the two big claws. When shut, they resembled giant spears that could easily pierce the hull of a combat rover. They opened, revealing their jagged edges. They closed over Al's ravaged corpse, pulling strands of meat and intestines to the mandibles under those big eye stalks.

Shaped like little spider legs, the mandibles frolicked, pulling the endless strands of intestine from Al's body like angel hair spaghetti from a pasta bowl. Above those mandibles were two large eyes that stood on four-inch-long stalks.

Roger's vision seemed to spin. He had seen a lot of weird creatures across the galaxy, some of which were difficult to describe. Yet, it was something that was oddly familiar—a strikingly *simple* organism—that struck him with a pulverizing fear that fried his nerves.

He was looking at a giant crab.

The eye stalks angled in his direction. Its claws recoiled, poised to lash out and strike as though he was only two feet away. It remained still, uncertain whether it wanted to abandon its meal in favor of the fresh one.

The clicking sound persisted, even though the crab remained in place. It grew nearer and nearer, eventually piercing through the fog of shock that kept Roger's eyes on the carnage.

He turned his eyes to the right, just in time to see a second giant crab. This one's attention was purely on him, a fact demonstrated by its outstretched claws and its fast approach.

"JESUS H. CHRIST!" Roger jumped backward, just barely avoiding the snap of those claws. The crab kept coming, its front legs tapping the edge of the ramp.

Roger pulled his sidearm from its holster and fired numerous rounds into the creature's face. Bright blue bullets, made of hot energy, burst against its shell. The crab lifted itself onto the ramp, completely unfazed by the projectiles.

Roger's frenzied mind went into a spin. In the split-second he had, he could only come up with one escape plan. He retreated into the ship, stopping briefly to reach for the ramp control. The crab scurried up the incline, its open claws forcing the co-pilot to retreat farther into the ship.

After a second futile attempt to repel the crustacean with blaster fire, Roger sprinted into the cockpit. He threw himself into the pilot's seat and prepped the spacecraft for emergency liftoff.

The crab crashed into the narrow doorway. Black eyes, like orbs on the end of small poles, angled in his direction. One of the claws reached into the cockpit, its pincer tips grazing the back of his seat.

"Oh, Jesus! Oh, God!" Roger squealed. He strapped himself in and pulled up on the yoke. The vertical thrusters lifted the dropship off the ground. In the intensity, he applied too much power to the engines, shooting the dropship nearly a thousand yards into the sky.

The crab was not ready to give up. Unable to reach its prey, it focused its wrath on the doorway. The steel frame crumpled under the vice-like grip of its pincers. Bit by bit, the crab widened the entrance.

Alarms blared across the ship. Red lights flashed in his face.

Through all of that sound, Roger was still able to detect the clicking of pointed feet *inside* the cockpit.

He looked over his shoulder, threw his arms over his eyes, and screamed as the pincers finally seized him.

A moment later, his arms no longer covered his eyes, for they had been pulled from his shoulders. The crab dropped the limbs in favor of pulling the rest of him apart.

The pincers rammed into his chest, cutting through flesh and bone.

Roger hung his head back, his scream a bloody gurgle. Still strapped in the chair, the armless pilot could only squirm as his chest was opened like the covers of a book, revealing the soft organs underneath.

The crab tore into him, shredding his body into unrecognizable chunks. The seat broke from its swivel and fell against the controls, deactivating the vertical thrusters.

The crab was too busy savoring the taste of human flesh to notice the freefall.

CHAPTER 9

The marines were in the process of docking the boat when they heard the sound of roaring engines. All eyes turned to the sky, where the dropship was inexplicably ascending at an alarming speed. It was lifted by its vertical thrusters, which appeared to be at full power.

"Jordan!" Walker said into his radio. "Report! What's going on?"

"Maybe the shore broke off?" Portman said.

"Then why aren't they saying anything?" Foreman said. "And why go that high?"

Richard completed docking and dropped the ramp. He and Milla hurried to the shore, their eyes glued to the bizarre sight above. From where they stood, the dropship appeared to be as small as a silver dollar.

It was a quarter-mile in the sky, teetering back and forth like a maritime vessel caught in a tropical storm. After a few moments, it leaned to starboard, the thrusters pushing it several dozen yards inland.

The thrusters went silent and the elevation came to an abrupt halt. In that same moment, the vessel descended into a freefall.

An astonished Stevie stumbled backward, his eyebrows nearly touching his hairline. "Uh... Sarge?!"

"Jordan! Grill! Goddamnit, what the hell's going on up there?!" Walker said.

For five painful seconds, the marines watched the fall. Elevation in the island's interior obstructed their view of the crash, but not of the sound. An eruption rivaling naval artillery shook the island. A plume of smoke and dust spat into the sky.

Walker shot into action, immediately racing into the compound. Richard followed him inside the lab area, where the fire extinguishers were held. Both men took two of them, then returned to the rest of the squad. Foreman and Milla each took one of the extinguishers and waited as the rest of the squad ran into the building to grab more. Knowing how flammable unstable core liquid was, they knew they would need as many extinguishers as possible. Judging by that cloud, the crash site was completely ablaze.

"Quinn, you stay here with the civilians," Walker said. "Keep working on resuscitating them. The rest of you, on me!"

Walker led his marines to the crash site with a hasty sprint. Within a few short seconds, that smoke plume had doubled in size. The energy core had likely ignited, spewing flames for only God knows how far.

Reaching the higher elevation of the island's center, the marines got their first view of the wreckage. As they feared, parts of the ship were everywhere. Hull, engine parts, equipment, seats, internal components, had been scattered for as far as the eye could see.

Fire blazed across the crash site, a thin blue light glistening where the core had burst. The flames, feeding off rivers of core fluid, danced as though in celebration of the recent death and destruction.

"It's gone," Portman said. "Look at this! The ship is destroyed. What the hell are we gonna do? We're stranded here."

"Portman, shut the fuck up and start putting out the flames," Walker said. The Sergeant slung his rifle over his shoulder and approached the nearest flames, which danced around what appeared to be the remains of the starboard engine. The rest of the squad joined in, starting with the initial wall of fire before fanning out to extinguish the rest.

***

"Heaven have mercy," Jerry said, watching the ever-expanding smoke cloud. It was as if the fires of hell had ripped from the island in a volcanic eruption. The cloud spread high in the sky, tinting the clear atmosphere with black soot. "That's unbelievable. What do you think happened?"

"More importantly, how the hell are we gonna get out of here?" Dante said.

"We'll worry about that later," Quinn said. "Will you guys help with this, for godsake?"

The engineers, having unloaded their equipment, assisted the medic in getting the three researchers off the boat.

Quinn took Sara McQuade by the arm and helped her to a bench near the dock shed. Still droopy-eyed, Sara tried to speak, only to be silenced as Quinn put a rebreather to her mouth and sat her near the shed.

"Shh. Relax. You were clinically dead for a minute," he said. He turned his eyes to the other two researchers. On the return trip, he learned their names. The one with the flask was Dr. Ben Cross, the station's medical officer. The other one, with a neat haircut and white lab coat, was Dr. John Kern, the man in charge of whatever studies were taking place here. Both men were still in a state of confusion following their resuscitation. In Ben's case, he was hazy and half-drunk.

Jerry and Dante sat them down on the ground near the bench.

"What… what happened?" John said, his voice barely above a whisper. "We heard an explosion."

"Don't concern yourself with that right now," Quinn said. "My team is handling it as we speak."

Dante scoffed. "Not sure what they can do except pick up the scraps." He shook his head and sighed in defeat. "We're totally screwed."

"Dante?" Quinn said. The engineer looked over at him. "Can you just do a small favor and shut up? That'd be great."

Dante ground his teeth, noticing Jerry shooting a glare in his direction. The sentiment was clear. *Yes, I agree.* With this in mind, Dante resumed watching the buildup of smoke and dust.

In that time, only one phrase escaped his lips.

"No ship. Island falling apart. Carnivorous sea-bugs running around on this island. What else could go wrong?"

***

The squad branched out and smothered the flames in a chemical mist. Little by little, the fire and heat subsided, the base of the smoke tower now thinning into a grey veil. As visibility increased, the marines laid eyes on the full extent of the wreckage. Debris and equipment had been scattered in all directions, some smoking hot from the fire, others miraculously untouched.

Stevie lowered his extinguisher nozzle. He was desperately fighting off an angry outburst. Just a few hours ago, he was resting peacefully in his pod, blissfully unaware of the existence of this planet. The last thing he remembered before then was prepping for the flight home. It had been a long two years on Rosseni. He, like the rest of his squad, was ready for a much-deserved vacation. It was bad enough his sleep was unexpectedly interrupted by this 'simple' pickup mission. Though resentful, he accepted the task. For all he knew, there would be a pay bonus involved. And how bad would visiting a rare ocean planet be, really?

As it turned out, this place sucked. There were too many unanswered questions. What happened to the crew? Why were the doctors hiding in a submersible? Why was it smashed up? He wasn't willing to bet those sea-mantid things Walker and Richard killed were responsible for all of this. Whatever caused the damage to that station clearly was much bigger.

The worst question was *How the hell are we gonna get off this planet?* Their ride was smashed beyond recognition, and the colony's shuttle was underwater. Their only chance was to contact a freighter and get a second rescue team out here.

There were two problems with that. First, the radio tower was heavily damaged and unable to put out calls. Second, the freighter was continuing on its voyage. This would not be a problem under normal circumstances. The dropship had plenty of capacity to catch up with it and dock. But even if the marines could get a call out, it would take the rescue team at least a few hours to get out here. By the time they arrived, it would be at least a day, and it did not appear this island would last that long.

Another tremor tested their balance while the marines put out the flames. Walker, true to form, kept his marines under control. One thing they had learned in training was not to lose their heads in a crisis. A panicked mind was not conducive in creating solutions.

"Keep yourselves together, men," he said. "First things first: sort through this shit. Take anything worth salvaging and bring it back to the station. Come on, let's move."

Stevie exhaled slowly, then placed his extinguisher down. He turned northward, where the bow section of the dropship appeared to have smashed. Perhaps, somehow, the radio components had survived the crash. The engineers would possibly be able to replace some wiring and get a signal out to the freighter. If they could repair it quickly, that would cut down on the response time.

He stepped around some smoking pieces of engine steel. Their grey fumes acted as a fog which permeated the air. Stevie entered the mist, quickly locating several large shapes that originally made up the front of the ship. The first segment was part of the nose, recognizable only by its pointed shape. Even that made it difficult to identify the fragment, for it was heavily dented and tattered.

The next piece section was part of the cockpit itself. Fueled by a sense of hopeful optimism, Stevie ran to the array of battered controls. Waving his hand, he brushed away some of the smoke, clearing the view of the instruments.

He had expected to see the frayed electronics and other signs of damage. What he didn't expect was the fresh wet blood that coated the console. It was fresh, having survived the crash and subsequent burning.

A few inches right of its center was the radio. Stevie checked the panel to see if he could remove it with the basic tools in his vest. As he figured, it would require the engineers to remove it from the rest of the wreckage. Though he was no expert in electronics, it at least appeared to be functional enough. Perhaps the hull had allowed the internal components to survive the crash. With a little luck, maybe they could get it to function.

Stevie turned to alert his squad. "Hey, guys—"

He stopped mid-sentence, his attention shifting to a strange, crackling sound. Whatever it was, it somewhat resembled cracking joints or clicking typewriter keys.

Stevie looked to the west. Three meters from his position was a large mass. He had seen it when he initially approached the cockpit and assumed it was part of the wreckage.

This 'wreckage' had eight pointed digits extending from its underbelly. Each one was segmented into three sections, each one connected by a flexible joint. Their ends were spear-tipped, appearing sharp enough to penetrate advanced body armor.

The huge mass they were attached to was bulky, yet somewhat flat. The edges were lined with spines, which were blue compared to the pale underside. At its front were two extra limbs which were bulkier than the others.

Arms. Arms *and* legs.

He was looking at a lifeform.

It was alien, yet strikingly familiar. The familiarity was also what made it so bizarre. He was looking at a crab. A giant, monster crab.

The creature shifted its body to one side, thrashing its legs and arms with intense might. The effort was successful in righting itself. The legs elevated its mass to the height of a quarter horse. At this point, its mass became fully apparent. Its body was as wide as an infantry personnel carrier, its weight at least eight hundred pounds.

Immediately, it set its sights on the dumbfounded marine. Its pincers raised above its head and opened, the left one sporting a blood-soaked piece of fabric.

Stevie recognized the insignia—it was a shred from a pilot's jumpsuit.

The marine shouldered his rifle and fired. The crustacean charged through the volley of plasma bolts, each one exploding uselessly against its shell. Its speed was as shocking as its size.

Stevie shrieked through clenched teeth as the creature closed the distance in a few short seconds.

Both pincers closed around his midsection, their edges pressing deep into his body. Stevie reared his head back, his shriek now a high-pitched wail. Lower ribs cracked, muscles split, and his spinal column bent inward.

The crab lifted him off the ground with minimal effort, its eyes watching its prey kick and squirm in its grasp.

Richard turned toward the sound of screaming. "Stevie?!"

"Go! Go! Go!" Walker bellowed.

The squad sprinted into action, crossing over a hundred feet of rock before arriving near the cockpit wreckage.

All at once, they came to a stop, each one shocked to see their fellow marine in the claws of a giant crab. Stevie had dropped his rifle, his training overridden by pain and horror. The crab slammed him into the ground, reducing the screaming to a heavy grunt.

The process of evisceration followed.

It angled one of its open claws straight downward and jabbed the tips into Stevie's midsection. Pain triggered a physical response. The marine's arms and legs shot upward while a vomiting sound erupted from his throat.

The marines took aim and fired.

"Kill it!" Foreman yelled.

Even as blaster bolts struck its side, the crab continued the cruel process of feeding. The claw snipped up Stevie's middle, strategically opening him up. The marine's head was flat, his tongue protruding from his outstretched mouth as his insides were promptly removed.

"Son of a bitch!" Portman yelled. "It's not even flinching."

"Shell's too thick," Richard said.

"Foreman!" Walker said. No order was needed. The heavy weapons specialist knew exactly what to do. Stevie was already on the brink of death, his stomach completely torn open and spread across the rocks. It was as though the crab enjoyed what it did. Rescue was futile, but payback was still on the table.

The marine pointed his grenade launcher at the fiend. "Snack on this, motherfucker."

He fired two projectiles, both of which exploded on impact. The crab flipped over, its legs kicking madly from the seemingly abrupt impact. Cursing, Foreman fired another pair of grenades which exploded against its underbelly. A shockwave traveled through its body, bringing its movements to a halt.

Foreman lowered the smoking muzzle and spat in the crab's direction. Stevie was dead, his body lying around rivers of his own blood which dripped over the rocks.

Walker approached with intent to remove the dog tags, only to immediately back away with his rifle shouldered.

"Heads up!"

Those legs kicked once more, this time with a ferocity that conveyed anger. The crab righted itself and turned to face the squad. No longer was its attention on its victim, but on the other marines.

It darted toward them, easily withstanding the bombardment of blaster bolts and grenades.

The marines backed away, but amazingly could not outpace the giant crustacean. With no other choice, they scattered. The crab rotated on its feet, pincers cocked and ready to lunge. It searched for a target, unperturbed by the pathetic strobes of light that struck its shell.

Its eyes settled on Portman. The marine had reloaded and was taking aim at its face. Several bolts struck near its left eye, the heat agitating the tiny nerves that ran through them.

Portman, realizing its attention was on him, started backpedaling.

The crab charged. The marine screamed in horror, his rifle blasting at full-auto. He may as well have thrown cotton balls at the beast.

"No, no, no, *no*! NO!!! GET AWAY FROM ME!!!"

Those huge claws seized him, one by the arm, the other by his leg. The wailing Portman kicked and screamed six feet above the ground, the pincers cracking his femur and humerus.

The crab slammed him to the ground.

For a split-second, the pain was gone, the world hazy. Portman was on his back, staring at the sky. The pressure on his shoulder ceased... and a whole new pain. The brief numbness disappeared, overpowered by the pain in his left leg. Both claws were going to work, one holding his hip down while the other pulled the limb from his body.

Portman gagged, his eyes bulging as he watched the flesh and tendons stretch and snap. The crab, unbothered by the gunfire that continuously struck its shell, munched on the severed leg as though it was a drumstick. The mandibles made short work of the limb, shredding meat and bone as though it was cotton candy. Once it got to the knee, it stuck the limb into its mouth and freed its claws.

With his boot sticking out of its mouth, the crab reached for Portman. Giant claws punctured his abdomen and sliced it open, revealing a pool of soft organs, intestines, and blood.

Richard neared the crab in an attempt to deter it. Several shots struck its shoulder, though the crab hardly noticed. It pulled guts from Portman's body and slurped them up.

Clicking and tapping sounds alerted the Corporal to another presence. He turned on his heels, gasping as he saw another huge crab advancing from the west.

"We've got another one!" he shouted.

This one was equally as large as its companion. Judging by the blood on its outstretched claws, equally as violent.

Now it made complete sense. These two crabs ambushed Al Jordan and Roger Grill, chasing them into the dropship, resulting in an emergency takeoff and ultimately the crash.

Its shell was as solid as the other's, easily withstanding the marines' weaponry.

Foreman hit the thing with a pair of grenades, momentarily halting its attack. The crab fell to its left, kicking its right legs in the air before correcting its posture.

"Fuck me," Milla said. "Nothing can hurt these things."

"Withdraw," Sergeant Walker said. It was an order he did not like to give, but he had no choice. They couldn't handle one of these creatures, let alone two of them. They were armored, violent, and agile. Standing toe-to-toe with them would only guarantee the death of every marine in this squad. "Everyone, back to the station. Move! Move! Move! Move! Move!"

***

The sound of rifle fire was endless, rivaling the full-scale conflicts of Nahawdi. The team had either encountered an entire swarm of those insectoid creatures, or something worse.

"The hell's going on?" Dante said.

"Get everyone inside," Quinn said.

"The station?" Jerry said, pointing at the damage. "Don't think so. We'd probably be better off on one of the boats."

Quinn gave the suggestion some consideration. "Yeah, good idea." He adjusted his helmet mic. "Sergeant, what's happening?"

As the medic awaited a response, Jerry rushed onto the boat's deck. Before getting everyone aboard, they needed to move the submersible to make room.

"Dante, help them to their feet," he said, pointing at the researchers. John Kern's senses seemed to return completely. He and Sara were looking to the sound of gunfire with dread in their eyes. A flood of memories were returning, none of them good.

"They're back," Sara said.

"What's back?" Dante said.

"The cr—" She looked to the boat ramp. The water near the starboard side rippled. "Get away from the boat!!!"

Jerry glanced at her. "Huh?"

The boat shuddered from a grazing impact. A series of scraping sounds followed as a rigid object brushed against the hull. He turned to look, fearing he would see more of those sea-bug creatures emerging from the water.

What he saw was far worse.

What he *felt* was excruciating pain.

Jerry Morgalo found himself in the clutch of a mammoth crab pincer. The beast, equal to the size of a rover, lifted the engineer off the ramp.

"Sweet Lord." Quinn pivoted to take aim at the beast. The researchers were on their feet and backpedaling inland.

"Shit! It's back!" Ben Cross yelled.

Sara gasped. "Oh God… Caesar…"

"What the hell is that?!" Dante shouted.

"What do you think?!" Sara said. "It's a giant fucking crab!"

Jerry pushed his palms against the claw in a futile effort to free himself. He threw his head back and squealed. The claw tightened, crushing his pelvis and hips. The engineer, flooded with pain, swayed back and forth. The other claw closed over his left shoulder and chest, stopping his writhing.

Both claws pulled in opposite directions. Jerry's body stretched, then split at the middle. Stomach, kidneys, liver, and intestines splattered onto the deck. The crab's eyes angled toward the other humans, as though it was aware of how vile and unnerving its actions were.

Dante covered his mouth. "Oh, God! Jerry!"

Quinn took aim with his rifle and fired. Several shots burst over its shell, hardly even leaving a burn mark. It stood and munched, its nonchalance almost coming off as mocking.

Its mandibles pulled Jerry's upper torso apart. Pausing with his entrails dangling from its mouth, the crab rotated on its eight thick legs and faced the boat.

Sara gasped. "Oh no... it remembers our escape."

The crab confirmed this fact by driving its claws through the hull of the boat. With raking motions, it carved a large breach through the starboard side. Internal components splintered under its wrath. The vessel's computer blared a warping alarm sound, indicating the fuel cell had been breached.

Quinn emptied his rifle into the creature's side, each shot equally as futile as the last. With the magazine battery spent, he opted for something with a little more kick. He pulled two of his grenades from his vest, activated them, and chucked them at the creature.

Two explosions rocked its shell. The crab leaned away from the blast, remained still for a moment, then turned toward the doctor.

In that moment, Quinn realized he should have just turned around and ran.

The beast darted at him with frightening speed and snatched him off the shore.

***

"This is ridiculous!" Milla shouted. "First mantids, now giant crabs?! Fuck this planet!"

"Stow it, Marine," Walker said. "Corporal, you have eyes on the bastards?"

Every few steps, Richard looked over his shoulder. The crabs delayed their chase in favor of feeding off Stevie and Portman's corpses.

"They're still back there," he said.

Gunshots from a plasma rifle echoed from the dock area. Two explosions followed, then intense screams.

Walker led the team to the dock area. First, they saw Sara, Dante, John, and Ben gathered together. They were backing toward the station, unable to take their eyes off the dock area.

The team crossed a large mound, which gave them a clear view of the dock area.

Richard felt his heart jump into his throat.

Near the boats stood a fourth monster crab. 'Monster' was the key word in this case. This crab was almost double the size of the others. This one nearly matched the size of a land-based assault vehicle.

In its grasp was Quinn. Even from this distance, they could see the blood spouting from his mouth. The screams had stopped, for his ribcage had been crushed into his lungs.

The crab almost seemed interested in its kill. It held Quinn up to one of its eyes, watching him spasm under its grip. After a short period of gazing, it lowered him to its mouthparts, which gleefully extended to accept him.

Milla gasped. "Oh no. Oh, Heaven! OH GOD!"

Quinn was delivered to its mouth and endured the agony of being eaten alive. His entire front half found its way into the creature's mouth. His legs kicked between the mandibles, which frolicked around them before tearing them apart.

Milla fell to her knees and vomited.

"Pull yourselves together, Marines," Walker said. "Foreman, hit that bastard."

The explosives specialist took the Sergeant's place. He aimed his freshly aimed grenade launcher thirty-degrees, then fired all six grenades. The six explosives fell at a perfect arch, bursting around the giant crustacean. Gravel and dust shot up, the target lurching from each blast. Like with the others, it was relatively unfazed by the blasts.

The sixth grenade landed between it and the boat. A dual-explosion followed, catching everyone, including the crab, by surprise. The research boat lifted out of the water and crashed down, the fuel cell having ignited. Hot blue flames spat from its hull, emitting thick toxic fumes.

Pincers slashed at the air. The crab, still munching on Quinn's lower half, darted to its left, snapping at the air as though somehow that would repel the smoke. Disinterested in the remaining humans, it backed into the water and submerged.

"It doesn't like fire," Foreman said.

"That doesn't make sense," Jac said. "It can handle the heat from our guns, but can't stand flames?"

Walker shook his head. "Not the flames. It's the smoke. NW-14 fuel cells emit toxic fumes when they burn."

"You think it kills them?" Milla asked.

"All we know is that it repels them," Richard said. "That's good enough for me."

"Me too," Walker said. He raised his voice so the civilians could hear him. "Everyone assemble at the station."

Ben Cross looked at him and threw his arms out. "And do what?! They'll tear the place apart!"

Walker approached the doctors, keeping one eye on the water in case the crab returned. "Do you have any spare fuel cells? In the maintenance shed, perhaps?"

Sara's jaw quivered as she tried to focus. "The drone station! Should have three or four to charge the drones."

A new tremor rocked the island.

"Like we don't have enough problems," Dante said.

Walker pointed at him. "You! Come with us. The rest of you, get to the station."

"Me? Why me?!"

"We need you to disassemble the energy compartment so we can get those fuel cells," Richard said.

"Come on, Dante!" Walker said. "Snap out of it. If we don't get those cells, we're all dead."

Dante quivered. After seeing that crab, he was unsure if he would ever approach a body of water ever again, let alone the shorelines on this godforsaken island. His fragile mind retained enough sense to know not getting those cells would leave them defenseless against those crabs.

"Alright, alright!"

Foreman and Jac led the scientists to the station, leaving Walker to lead the rest of the team to the east shore.

It was a relatively short run, unhindered by the presence of crabs.

Walker goaded Dante to the drone maintenance building. They went through the door and found the charging station.

Another tremor rippled beneath their feet.

"Act fast, Dante," Walker said. "Can you access those cells or not?"

"Y-yes," the jittery engineer said. His nerves were still fried from seeing his supervisor torn apart. He reached into his tool kit and found the drill.

Each section of the station had its own panel where the cells were stored. He knelt to the one on the right and retracted the screws.

Richard and Milla stepped outside to give him room. Both kept their eyes to the west. Somewhere behind that elevation were two murderous crabs.

A third tremor struck the island.

Waves crested and smashed against the shore.

Deep, crunching vibrations echoed from under the ground. Richard and Milla looked down, then at each other. Right then, the earth shifted.

A crack in the rock emerged several yards inland. In that moment, the marines realized they were riding a chunk of the shoreline out to water.

"Sarge! We've got new problems," Richard said.

Walker could feel the shift from inside. "Here! We've got the first two. Take them!" He passed two fuel cells to his marines. The cylinder-shaped cells shone bright blue. Richard double-checked the seals to make sure they were on tight.

Dante got to work on the third.

Another tremor began parting the chunk of land. The shoreline began to tilt, forcing the marines to shift their balance.

"Sarge! We've got to go!" Richard said.

Walker passed the third one to him.

"Get that last one, Dante!"

Dante was already on it. The drill went to work. One screw fell free. Then another. Then the third. Then… "Shit! Shit! Shit! This one's jammed."

"Get out," Walker said. He grabbed the engineer by the collar and threw him out of the shed. "All of you, get across the split."

Richard looked at the rising water. "But Sergeant…"

"Damn it, Corporal, that's an order."

The fireteam obeyed his instructions. Richard followed Dante over the newly-formed crevice, glancing into the abyss. The ocean was already claiming this chunk of land, filling the void between it and the rest of the island.

The broken section of shoreline, stretching for hundreds of feet, leveled out and began to sink.

Inside the shed, Walker took aim at the last screw on the panel. Several shots broke the final screw away, separating the panel and uncovering the fuel cell. It was a risky solution. The hot energy had nearly burned its way to the cell, stopping centimeters short.

Walker removed the cell and stepped out. The water was at his ankles now and steadily rising.

"Corporal!" He tossed the fuel cell to Richard.

The marine caught it, then set it down in favor of his rifle. "Sarge! Behind you!"

Walker knew that could only mean one thing. He turned his head just in time to see the threat. Sure enough, it was another crab.

This one was roughly as large as the others. One distinct feature separated it from the others: the bottom pincer on its left claw was broken off, rendering the limb as a javelin.

The handicap did not deter the crustacean, which struck with mantis-like speed.

The broken claw speared the Sergeant, its tip bursting out his back. Straightening its legs, the crab lifted its victim from the water, snapping its other claw with intent to dismember him.

Even under intense pain, even with blood dripping from his mouth, Walker refused to yell out, nor did he give the crab the satisfaction of displaying pain. If there was anything he learned about this new enemy, it was that they savored their kills.

He pulled his Shipley-92 plasma pistol from its holster and fired into the crab's face.

The shoreline sank, taking the crab and the Sergeant with it. Before they vanished, the crab put its right claw to Walker's neck.

SNAP!

There was nothing Richard and Milla could do but watch as their Sergeant was decapitated. His headless body, still skewered by its captor, disappeared under the water.

The tremors ceased, the bloody water slowly calming down.

"Oh, man..." Dante said. "They got the Sarge. They—they got the Sarge!"

"Shut up," Richard said.

Two realities sank in: Sergeant Walker was dead, something nobody ever thought was possible. And now Richard Carson was in charge, a responsibility he absolutely did not want.

Fate had a way of choosing terrible circumstances to reveal itself.

He knew he could not stand here any longer. He needed to figure out a plan, and he needed to do it fast. With that in mind, he issued his first order.

"Back to the station."

CHAPTER 10

The news of Sergeant Walker's demise went as well as expected. Foreman and Jac, marines who were tough as nails, were visibly shaken. They had all lost people before. It was the way of things. A vast expansion always meant conflict was on the horizon. But Sergeant Lou Walker? They thought such a man could not be killed by anything except old age.

Not only was the Sarge gone, but so was half of their squad. In just a matter of minutes, this stupid 'simple' operation had resulted in the destruction of their transport, the death of two pilots, one engineer, and four marines. The enemy was different than anything they had ever encountered.

Crabs, of all things. That single reality was almost as mindboggling as the Sergeant's death.

The first plan of action was defense. The marines collected whatever scrap they could find and welded them over the breaches. They all knew it was a futile effort, but it was better than doing nothing. Hardly anyone looked to Richard for guidance. He did not take offense, for it was not a responsibility he desired. As time went on, he hardly issued a single order. The decision to barricade the station was a collective one. It was an opportunity for the marines to digest their current situation.

As time passed, the station smelled of burned metal.

If there was anything good that came from this period of fortifying, it was that no crabs showed up.

Yet.

Richard stood with Milla in the front lounge area. On the floor was the equipment they had managed to salvage from the wreckage. The machine gun managed to survive thanks to the durability of its steel case. Inside were two large battery drums with a capacity of three hundred level-three caliber plasma bolts. Aside from that, only a couple of rifles and battery mags were found.

"You alright with keeping watch?" Richard said.

"You asking me or telling me?" Milla said. She already knew the answer. Not in the mood to deal with the Corporal's crippling indecisiveness, she spared him the strain of giving an answer. "Yes, *Corporal*, I'll take watch. If anything arrives, you'll be the first to know."

Richard nodded his appreciation, then disappeared into the hall. The sound of welding and cursing intensified as he neared the lab. Foreman and Jac were hard at work sealing the entry points to the best of their ability. Pieces of scrap taken from the boats, wreckage, and storage shed were placed across the breaches and welded to the walls.

Seated at one of the tables were the three doctors. Ben Cross had a bottle of whiskey in front of him. Remarkably, it remained unopened. The reason for this became obvious when Richard saw Sara's face. He knew the look she had when she chastised anyone for doing something stupid. Clearly, she had just finished laying into the doctor for his willingness to dull his senses in a time of crisis.

"Everyone alright?" Richard asked.

"Could be better," Ben said, his eyes fixed on the bottle of whiskey. "Would have preferred to suffocate peacefully, but nooo…"

Richard ignored the statement and shifted his attention to John and Sara. "What about you two?"

"Well, all things considering…" Sara said.

"I'm sorry we didn't warn you," John said. "Last thing I remember, we were watching through the submarine window. Then black. All of a sudden, I'm on a boat. And even that's a blur. By the time my wits returned, all hell was breaking loose again."

"What exactly happened?" Richard said.

Jac chuckled. "'What happened?' he says. "I think it's pretty clear what happened here. Big crabs showed up, wrecked the place, and killed everybody. That's what happened."

"No shit," Foreman said.

Richard kept his attention on the doctors. "Have you seen these creatures prior to the attack?"

Sara shook her head. "Before the seismic activity began, no. Several days after the first big earthquake, we noticed a drastic change in the local sea life. Several creatures had gone missing. I didn't think much of it at first. I figured some of the larger animals were seeking new habitats after the disturbance. Then, while using our drones for geologic surveying assignments and sampling, I discovered the remains of a large leridox, a local species of whale.

"Its bones were broken, including its skull. Most of the flesh had been consumed. It was not there two days prior. A few days later, I went to retrieve one of our drone drillers. It would not respond to my transmitter, so I had to use the minisub to get it. When we retrieved it, it was crushed beyond recognition. There were narrow abrasions, as though crushed by a..." she chuckled "...I guess I can say *a crab claw.*"

"Fast-forward to later," John said. "We set out a call for help, started prep for evac, getting computer chips and samples. Then, out of nowhere, we hear screams. We check. There they were, eating our maintenance crew. We tried to hide inside and contacted our shuttle pilots to not leave their shacks. Over time, they tore up the place and got in. Destroyed our radio equipment, killed Jess, Monty, Taka, our lab assistants—everybody."

"The three of us, with one other person, managed to get to the boats," Sara said. "One of the crabs chased us out. It clung to the boat and held on. We tried to shake it off, but no such luck. It started making its way aboard." She closed her eyes and took a deep breath. "Our nurse, Isaac Lee, was good with boats. The stupid safety system required the boat to be anchored before the crane could be operated. He dropped the anchor and activated the crane."

"Sacrificed himself," Ben muttered. His desire for that whiskey overcame his fear of Sara McQuade. He opened it and filled his flask.

"On our way down, we were attacked by a hawk eel," Sara said. "It was probably drawn to the water distortion. They're big, highly aggressive creatures with huge beaks. This one was especially large. Wrecked the rudder. It eventually gave up and swam away, but we were unable to go anywhere. To make matters worse, the crabs eventually tracked us down. They tried to rip the submarine apart. The only way we managed to drive them off was by drawing power from the cell and producing a high-voltage electrical flash through the outer hull. Took a few tries, but the crabs lost interest."

She went ahead and took a sip from the whiskey bottle. "That's about the gist of what happened."

"You never saw them until after the first major earthquake?" Richard said. "Is it possible they're not originally from this particular area?"

"I think that's the case," Sara said. "I suspect they're deep-dwelling crustaceans, used to harsher water pressures. I think thermal activity in the deep may have driven them to the surface. Their claws are evolved to kill other crustaceans and dig through hard rock to chase prey from their burrows."

Foreman lowered his welder and turned toward the scientists. "Thermal activity?"

John nodded. "That was one of the purposes of our research project. Between the crust and mantle is a radioactive geothermal reservoir. Not magma, but rather an oily layer of hot fluid similar to the Titanus-mons fluid we use in our power cells. Except, based on our studies, a single cannister of this stuff would outlast fifty standard power cells."

"The most easily assessable deposit is here," Sara added.

"Lovely," Jac said. "So, to sum it up, the Assembly wants to turn this planet into a big oil well."

"Takes fuel to traverse the galaxy," John said.

"Do you know how many of them there are?" Jac asked.

Sara gave him a bitter glance. Again, her face said it all. John Kern was a good, considerate man who valued the lives and safety of his people. But when it came to the ethical issues of mankind tearing up ecosystems for his own good, he hardly batted an eye.

Richard had looked at the file notes in the briefing room. John was the leader behind another energy alternative which fell through, taking his reputation and finances with it. This was an opportunity to be renowned as a hero by the Assembly, as well as be highly compensated for his discovery.

Still, the guy could never have predicted an attack by giant crabs. But, looking at him, Richard suspected the scientist would gladly lead an organized effort to eradicate all life around the deposit just to guarantee direct access.

"Any idea how many crabs are hunting around this island?" Richard asked.

"My estimation—four," Sara said. "I've noticed distinct characteristics and markings."

"She gave them pet names," Ben said.

"Nicknames," she said. "Helps with identifying them. There's Lance. He's got a broken claw, which makes his left arm act as a spear."

Richard nodded. Images of Walker's demise flashed in his mind. "We've met him."

"There's the brothers," Sara continued. "I call them Cliff and Klin, after a couple of names from some literature I've read in my childhood. Anyways, those two always travel and hunt together."

"Probably the two that attacked Al and Roger," Jac said.

"Did one of them have a stumpy back leg?" Sara asked. Richard nodded. "Then that's them for sure."

"What about the really big one?" Richard asked. "The one that killed Jerry and Quinn?"

Sara let out a long sigh. All three doctors leaned against the table. Just the mention of that thing seemed to fry their nerves.

"Caesar," John muttered.

Sara scoffed, her head resting on her palm. "You think the other ones are hard to kill? Try that freaking thing. It's practically a tank. The other crabs seem to act on its will. I actually witnessed the brothers bringing it food at one point."

"Seems like odd behavior for crabs," Foreman said.

"On Earth, maybe," Sara said. "Here on Challenger? For all we know, they're the dominant species. And I think they know it. I mean, Jesus, they almost seem to take pleasure in dismembering their victims."

"I can second that," Jac said. He tossed his welder onto the nearest table and approached Richard. "Carson, I'm not wasting any more time with useless barricades. These'll hold the crabs off for a minute at most. It's time for solutions. We need to get off this rock. Use one of the boats, maybe."

"None of them are functional," Richard said.

"Can't sit here and do nothing," Jac said.

"Hear-hear," Foreman said.

"Dante!" Jac said. The engineer was seated at a table near the east wall. He had his head in his hands, barely fending off a mental breakdown. Jac walked closer to him. "Dante!"

The engineer raised his head and his voice. "What?!"

"Snap out of it, dude," Jac said. "Listen, there's only one thing we can do. I need your help in repairing the radio tower."

Dante nearly sprang from his seat as though struck by a bolt of lightning. "Repair the radio tower. Have you *seen* the radio tower?! It's fallen over. How the hell are we gonna repair it?!"

"We'll use the crane to get it upright," Jac said. "We can weld supports on the legs to keep it standing. After that, we can repair the damage to the junction box. If we can get a signal out to the *Banning* we can get a shuttle out here. Get up. Let's get to it."

"That's a shit ton of repair work that would normally require a full team of engineers," Dante said.

"You suggesting you'd rather sit around and do nothing?" Jac said. Dante bit his lip, then shook his head. Reality had a way of hitting hard. "Then you better get to it. I'll help you out. I know a little bit about electronics. Come on."

Jac, Foreman, and Dante went for the hallway, not even offering Richard a glance, yet alone getting his approval for the plan.

"Hang on a sec," Richard said.

The marines stopped, their impatience plain on their faces.

"What's the problem?" Jac said.

"This island might not last long enough for rescue to get here," Richard said.

"Hence we're getting started now," Jac said. "In fact, we should have gotten to work on this right away. The longer we wait, the more likely we'll be here to watch the island sink. We don't have time to discuss this, Carson. There's no alternative. Our ship is destroyed. We're without a way off this island, let alone this planet. The freighter's moving farther away as we speak."

"Wait…" Ben Cross stuck his tongue out, his last sip of booze going down the wrong pipe after hearing that last sentence. "The freighter is still on route to its destination? Why can't it just drift?"

"It's an A-Class star freighter," Jac said. "You realize how much power it takes to shut down one of those engines and restart it? Maybe had we known we'd be arriving on Crustacean Planet, we would have awoken the ship's crew, but alas, we *didn't*!"

Ben raised his hands in surrender, then returned to his vice.

"What about the station's shuttle?" Richard said. "We originally planned to try and raise it from the water. It's only been submerged for a few days. The hull is meant to withstand the vacuum of space. It certainly can handle exposure to water for a limited time."

Jac shook his head. "The shuttle's on the other side of the island, which has been breaking away piece-by-piece for days. For all we know, the shuttle's buried under a bunch of rock. Even if we can locate the ship, we don't know if we can even lift it out of the water."

"Or if the hull is breached," Foreman added.

"Also, going to the south shore makes us prime targets for the crabs and whatever else is lurking out there," Jac said. "It's suicide. A dumb plan that'll get us killed. Not happening." He leaned toward the Corporal, his brow furrowing. "Not again."

He turned and went into the hall, Foreman and Dante right behind him.

Richard stood in his place, saying nothing while watching the marines walk through the hall. His rank had been reduced to a formality in their eyes. Six months ago, it was different. He had their respect.

Then came the standoff at Cerato Rock.

Richard felt the three pairs of eyes inquisitively watching him from the table. It was as though the doctors were looking to him for answers. Then again, how could they not? He was technically the leading rank in the group now, and their lives were at stake. He could feel their confidence waning over the next few seconds. Richard's mind was in a tug-of-war. His big mistake at Cerato Rock had shaken his confidence completely. At this point, Richard just wanted to wait the situation out. After all, the marines had already decided what they wanted to do. To hell with Richard's opinion.

For all he knew, they were right.

"Well, we're utterly fucked," Ben Cross said.

That remark was the final straw for Richard's stressed mind. Without saying a word, he marched into the hall and took a left turn to the radio room. The other marines were just now heading outside through the barricades. The coast was clear, giving them a window of opportunity to repair the tower.

Richard took a seat in the radio room. For the next moment, all he wanted was to appreciate the silence for a minute or two. As it turned out, he only got three seconds.

Approaching footsteps made him lift his head from the table. His blood rushed as he saw Sara arrive in the doorway.

The two stared at each other in dead silence, neither knowing exactly what to say.

Sara broke the ice with the simplest of phrases. "Hi."

"Hi."

She smiled nervously, slowly stepping inside. Her eyes went to the floor while her next words took form.

"I, uh, I guess I should thank you. You know? For saving our lives."

"You already did," Richard said. He wiped a bit of dust from the computer table. "Not that it's really necessary."

"No, it is," she said. She looked at the way he sat at the desk. Sara was good at reading body language. Looking at him, she noticed a smidge of longing in the way he sat. "Did they... reassign you? After... you know..."

"Cerato Rock. Yes, I know," Richard said. "We both know all too well. They put me on desk duty. Clerical-type stuff. Didn't bounce me back to private. Nah, they wanted the guys at home to do that. Sorry if that disappoints you."

"I... no! That's not..." Sara put her hands on her hips and looked up. A deep breath filled her lungs, her frustration spewing out with the exhale. "Forget it."

"Believe me, I'm trying."

Another set of footsteps came up the hall. This time, it was John Kern who joined them in the radio room.

"Sorry, am I interrupting?" he said.

"No," Richard said. "How are you feeling, Doctor?"

"Better, now that I'm out of that lounge," John said. "Couldn't take much more of Ben's pessimism. Guy's all doom and gloom."

"Like that's anything new," Sara said.

"True," John said.

"Cracking under pressure?" Richard asked. "Or just addicted to the bottle?"

"A little of both," John said. "It's a long story. Probably not my business to tell…"

"This is pretty much the only kind of work he can get," Sara said.

Richard flinched. "Isn't he a medical doctor?"

"Yeah, but his license has been knocked down to a 4-E," Sara said. "Basically, he can only work in prison colonies or outskirt research facilities like this one. Back in the day, he was a great physician. Then came the night of the black aurora."

"The EMP that struck the colony on Helios?"

Sara nodded. "He got called in. By then, he'd already downed a few cold ones, but being confident in his skills, didn't bother to tell anybody. Long story short, he severed a patient's artery. The woman died on the table. He's been a wreck ever since."

Richard glared at her. There was a reason she told that story, and it was not because she thought he was eager to know Ben's background.

"Corporal, how long would a flight from the freighter take?" John said.

"At this point? Between two and four hours, maybe."

John pointed his thump in the direction of the radio tower. "And by the time they get that thing fixed?"

"*If* they get it fixed," Sara said.

Richard sighed. "Eight or nine hours flight time."

"On top of the time it takes for them to fix it," John said. He leaned against the wall and shut his eyes. They were looking at a twelve-hour waiting period at minimum.

"What about the Corporal's alternative?" Sara said. "Is it possible we can raise our shuttle and fly ourselves out of here?"

John shrugged. "I'm no engineer. I wouldn't know if the engines were functional or not. Hell, that man Jac may be right. The shuttle might be crushed under five tons of rock for all we know."

Both of them looked at the Corporal.

Richard watched his reflection in the monitor. In the corner, he could see the scientists watching him, looking for answers. Even Sara, who had every reason in the universe to hate him, was depending on him for survival.

"Doctor Kern," he said. "How much longer do you think this island will last?"

John dug his hands into his pockets and pondered the rate of fragmentation that occurred over the last week.

"It had been sporadic for a while since the south shore broke away," he said. "For the next few days, it was little bits and pieces. The last several hours, though, the rate of disintegration has increased drastically. It's hard to say for sure how much longer it'll last."

"Twelve, thirteen hours?" Richard said.

"Maybe." John bit his lip, not wanting to complete that dreaded phrase. "Maybe not."

Richard looked to his reflection again. That face on the screen spoke to him with a tone harsher than all of his fellow marines combined.

It's all on you, you useless jackass. Gonna be a wangless coward, or are you going to trust your gut?

The internal chastisement did not inspire confidence. The last time he did go with his gut, innocent people died.

Including Sara's brother, the internal voice said. *You gonna let her die too? Jac's way will take too long. It might not work at all, and you know it.*

Richard stood up.

"There's a way we can find out." He strutted through the front lounge, passing Milla on the way to the makeshift doorway they'd created in the barricades.

"Got a plan?" she asked.

"Maybe." Richard stepped outside and found the others near the radio tower. "Dante! I'm gonna need the controls to your recovery drone."

The bewildered engineer looked at him. "My drone? Why?"

"We're using it for surveillance. It is functional, is it not?"

"Well, yeah. It was far enough away from the boat explosion. The control tablet was left by the boat shed."

"Good."

Jac watched the Corporal turn westward. "What are you doing, Carson?"

"Like you care to know," Richard muttered. He grabbed one of the power cells and headed for the docks.

Sure enough, Sara was right behind him. In her hand was one of the Hunter-Killer rifles salvaged from the crash. He almost laughed at the sight. Not because she looked clumsy with the gun—as a matter of fact, she looked like a pro—but because she used to complain about him constantly taking her to the shooting range on Rosseni.

"You should stay here," he said.

"Or, you can let me come along," she replied. "Someone's gotta watch your back."

Richard shook his head and kept going. "Fine. Not like anyone's following my orders today anyway."

CHAPTER 12

Propelled by water jetted from its syphon, the large cephalopod traveled east. The thunderous vibrations that drove so many other species away managed to attract the large predator. The reshaping of the seabed was to its liking, for it was becoming a jagged, mountainous area with plenty of places to hide. Intelligent and patient, it was the type of predator that usually preferred to ambush prey.

Its mantle was ten feet from its rear fins to its beak. Its six arms were over triple that, stretching to thirty-two feet. Made of pure muscle, those arms were capable of crushing the skull of a sixty-foot iron whale. The cephalopod was the only creature in this ocean that kept those whales from achieving the rank of apex predator.

For its own sustenance, the cephalopod preferred smaller prey. Lurking in the reefs near the west hemisphere islands, it enjoyed ambushing fish, lobsters, and sometimes other species of squids. There was no moral consideration for where its protein came from. It was a predator first and foremost, as even its own siblings had learned the hard way in the days following their birth.

It crossed the deep gorges and approached the shallows. The seabed steepened as it neared the island. Sprawled across the bottom were large rock fragments, providing plenty of hiding spots.

The cephalopod chose not to explore, rather drawn to water distortions in the shallows. Ascending the slope, it identified the source of the movement as being a small swarm of mantids. They were gathered on a section of rock that was leveled out, leading into the northeast shoreline. Little scavengers, they were picking at tiny scraps that accumulated in the area, totally oblivious to the new arrival.

Gently, the cephalopod clung to the bottom. Using its tentacles, it gently crawled in their direction, its frontmost arms coiled and ready to strike. Its color shifted, allowing it to blend with its environment. As far as the mantids were concerned, it was just another rock that was inexplicably moving in their direction.

Only when a few of their members were snatched by the tentacles did the colony realize the danger. The two unlucky mantids dug at the arms with their forelegs, failing to cut into the thick leathery skin. Their attempts to bite also proved futile, despite the ferocious cutting power of their mandibles.

Its beak, shaped like that of a parrot, opened wide and clamped down on the first mantid. The shell imploded, rupturing the crustacean's insides. Tasting the delicious blood, the cephalopod proceeded to suction the meat from the shell. The result was a thin, transparent exoskeleton being tossed aside.

It fed on its second victim in the exact same manner. Vacuuming the meat from the exoskeleton, the cephalopod crawled toward the shoreline. A few mantid fragments lay near a large rock. They were mostly legs, with a few sections of carapace and abdominal regions. Whatever killed these creatures was much more violent in its methods.

Though it preferred to hunt, the hungry cephalopod was happy to scavenge. Even the legs contained a tiny bit of meat. It moved toward the waterline, its mantle now grazing the surface.

It reached for one of the severed legs...

Snap!

Pain surged through its front-right tentacle. The 'rock' stood on eight legs, holding onto the squid with its pincer. The cephalopod jetted water. Its body waved like a kite, its outstretched arm acting as the string.

The Caesar crab held tight, making sure not to apply too much pressure. Severing the tentacle would sacrifice a large meal. He grabbed with its other claw and pulled the frenzied squid closer.

By now, the cephalopod knew escape was impossible. Only offensive measures provided an opportunity for survival. Redirecting its body, it lashed with its other five arms with intent to pin the giant crab, crack its shell, and bite at its joints.

Those arms wrapped around the crab's carapace and began to squeeze. The constriction, which had brought death to larger organisms than this foe, failed to compress this shell. There was no crack, no buildup of pressure, not even a hint of alarm from the crab itself. The crustacean calmly fixed its grip, snapping its claws shut over the mantle.

Nerves fired throughout the cephalopod's body. Its tough flesh, tougher than the shells of some crustaceans, peeled effortlessly under the edge of those pincers. The squid released its grip and blew another stream of water from its syphon. Its body remained in place, pinned by the crab's superior strength. Tentacles wrapped around its claws and arms, only to be snipped away.

Caesar now had a firm grip on the mantle, allowing him to feed at his leisure.

Arms flailed, the squid twisting and turning. Any sense of strategy disappeared. For the first time, the creature had experienced the surprise of being ambushed, and the agony of being eaten alive.

***

"Whoa!" Richard put his hand on Sara's shoulder and pushed her down. "Shh!"

She crouched beside him and watched. The water beside the remains of the dock were thrashing. Long blue tentacles rose from the water, coiling like earthworms in distress. Purple blood and ink distorted the otherwise clear water, obscuring the struggle taking place beneath.

Caesar's back was visible, resembling a spiny mountain standing in a stormy sea.

The crab stood tall, its pincers snapping at his prey. Pieces of flesh peeled off of the unfortunate squid.

"Do these things ever stop eating?" Richard said.

"No," Sara replied. "They require a hell of an appetite."

"Well, they've found it here," Richard said.

They remained in place, quietly watching the struggle ensue. The tentacles, spewing blood from the stubs where they had been severed, quivered and coiled. As death took hold, the squid-creature appeared to deflate, its limbs wilted and blobbed.

Caesar, now victorious, began to feed on his victim. He lifted one of the tentacles to its mandibles, which broke down the tough flesh with ease. The crab worked its way down to the webbing between the tentacles, then suddenly retracted its jaws. More snipping followed.

"The hell's it doing?" Richard asked.

Sara winced as a round sac was removed from under the squid's webbing and tossed aside.

"Poison sacs," she said. "Caesar knows that if he eats those, he's a goner."

"Son of a bitch," Richard said. "The bastard's that smart?"

Sara smirked and pointed at the feasting. "You saw it for yourself, didn't you?"

Richard turned his eyes back to the display of maritime carnage taking place before him. The crab removed a few more of the sacs and tossed them aside before resuming its meal.

Another 'mountain' rose from the water. It was smaller than Caesar, though sporting a similar color and shape. Sure enough, it was one of the other crabs.

Richard sneered as he saw the broken claw extend from the surface.

Lance.

Caesar dropped his prey and postured into an aggressive stance. Both claws reared back, ready to snap at the smaller crab. Lance, interested in the slain cephalopod, inched forward. Caesar, not keen on sharing, snapped at his subordinate. Lance scurried backward, the claws shutting less than a foot from his own arms. Getting the hint, the crab backed away, though continued to watch his master feast on the tentacled meal.

Caesar, growing increasingly impatient, grabbed his meal and backed away into deeper waters. The persistent Lance followed, clinging to the hope of salvaging a piece.

"I swear, if I could, I'd construct a giant pot and boil these fuckers to death," Richard said.

Sara stood up and pointed at the shed. "I see the drones... hey!"

Richard pushed her back down. "Shh! Quiet. Not sure if the others are still around."

"I'd think we'd know," Sara said, pushing his hand away. "The drone is right there. If we wait too long, they might get curious and try to eat it." She watched Richard shake his head. "What? This was your idea?"

"I'm just being cautious."

"No, you're being indecisive," she said. She stood up and strutted for the dock area.

"Sara… damn it." Richard stood up and went after her. "Sara, slow down. Follow my lead."

"What lead?" she said. "You're willing to let your marines walk all over you. The only reason you came to any decision at all is because Dr. Kern and I came to you."

"Listen, Sara… hey!" He stepped in front of her, stopping her. "You can pretend to be mad about that, or address the real issue. Listen, I can only say I'm sorry so many times for what happened on Rosseni. The fact is, *if* we get off this rock, you won't have to see my face ever again. It was a dumb stroke of luck that I was even awoken with the team. The ship's computer was unaware that I was disbanded from combat duty. It's not every day people are dragged out of cryosleep on a whim."

Sara looked him in the eye. A pitiful stare pierced his soul. Looking at him brought back so many memories. Some good. Some really good. Then one that was outright horrible.

"Listen, you saved my life," she said. "Trust me, you coming on this planet was a net positive as far as I'm concerned. Now, if we may…" she gestured toward the drone, "…there's more pressing matters at hand than our past. In case you've forgotten, we're on a sinking island roaming with giant man-eating crabs."

Richard ran a hand through his hair and stepped aside. "No, I haven't forgotten."

They walked in silence to the drone. Aside from some mild scarring from the explosion, it was undamaged.

Sara looked south along the shoreline. A couple hundred feet down was a fairly large ridge overlooking the water.

"That's a good spot to operate the drone from. We'll be able to see the crabs coming from any direction if they decide to pay us a visit."

"Fine with me," Richard said. "Does that remote's signal have enough range to direct the drone?"

"Yep. It's got a range of one-point-five miles," Sara said. "It's designed to go deep. Fortunately, the shuttle is only three-fourths of a mile away."

She activated the drone, then deployed it into the shallow water. After steering it farther out, she and Richard sprinted for the tall ridge. There, Richard stood guard while Sara operated the device.

During its travel, she kept it at surface level. The crabs were incapable of swimming, thus would be incapable of reaching the drone.

Richard glanced between the water and the screen. The drone moved at a remarkable speed. Being a recovery machine, it was capable of reaching its maximum depth in just a few minutes.

"Geez," Sara muttered.

"What's the matter?" Richard said.

"The ocean floor around the island is completely jacked up. There's a huge gorge just east of us. That's probably where the quakes are originating from."

"Is that a problem?"

Sara gave a sarcastic, toothy grin and nodded. "Seeing as it wasn't there a few days ago, I'd say yes. Dr. Kern is right. It's highly possible the seismic activity will intensify as the day goes on."

Richard saw the big split in the underwater landscape. The camera panned west, displaying the miniature mountain range comprised of the original shoreline. The island itself appeared to be standing on a shelf overlooking the seabed. It was an odd sight, almost giving the island a mushroom shape.

Aside from a few mantids, the area was void of life. They could see far in the distance, the sun's rays giving a false impression of a tranquil ocean.

The drone reached the southeast edge of the island. Serrated edge was a more adequate description. There was no smooth shore gradually leading into deeper water. The ground dropped off right as the water touched the island. Down below were heaps of rock that, until days ago, proudly served as a safe haven for land-dwelling organisms.

Sara exhaled slowly, nervous about what she would find. The 'search' part of this mission had officially begun.

She pushed the right joystick up, aiming the drone down at a forty-five-degree angle. Straight down was a collection of landmass that was all too familiar. Even in its broken-up state, she recognized some of the features she used to visit during her downtime.

There was the twisting cone, an odd, pointed rock formation that resembled an upside-down stalagmite. "The Big Fang", she used to call it. Then there was a large pan-shaped section where they had set up some basketball hoops. She could see parts of the metal poles lying several meters ahead. It had snapped in half, probably after having a chunk of island come down on top of it.

Thoughts of the good times brought a smile to her face, only to be reminded of what eventually came of her friends. She had left Rosseni to escape death, only to be faced with it again.

As though to offer another reminder, the water rippled where Caesar had disappeared. More blood and ink clouded its surface. The crab was enjoying his feast. Somewhere down there, Lance was probably picking away at some scraps.

Richard looked down the barrel of his rifle, sweeping it in every direction in search of any unwelcome crustaceans. So far, they were alone on this ridge.

"Let's move it along, please," he said.

"I'm looking," she said.

"Not all that hard," he said. "Gosh, how freaking hard is it to find a sixty-foot spaceship?"

Sara gritted her teeth, ready for her next comeback. A little smirk took shape instead, for this brief back-and-forth reminded her of a funny argument back on Rosseni.

"You remember the trip to Ridley Canyon?"

Richard nodded. "The trip that almost made me late for duty."

"That aqua-blue rover I used to drive," she added. "Remember that?"

"Yes," he said. "I know what you're getting at. How you drove us out there and you forgot where you parked the damn thing. How you couldn't find that stupid blue thing in the middle of that canyon, I'll never know."

"Hey, you couldn't find it either," she said.

"You're the one who dragged my sorry ass out there," he said. "Thought I was gonna be lunch for some dust maggots for a second. Nope… just big crabs seven months later." Sara scoffed. "I guess I'm nothing but bad luck for you, huh?"

"You were that day at the canyon," he said. Two smiles followed the statement. One from him, the other from her.

The banter took them back to simpler times. Times that now seemed trivial compared to the current struggles they were faced with.

Sara moved the drone around. "Ah-ha! Found it!"

Richard leaned toward the screen. There it was, the Y-engine passenger shuttle. The two cylinder-shaped ion engines were partially obscured by rock and sediment. The bow section, however, was completely visible. The front visor was completely intact, the hull integrity appearing to be uncompromised. The hatches were sealed with no signs of irreparable damage.

"The cockpit seems fine," Richard said.

"From what I can see," Sara said. "But if we do manage to raise the ship, who would fly it? The station pilots are dead, you guys lost yours…"

"I can get us in the air," Richard said.

"You can fly?"

"Needed something to do in my spare time after the—never mind. Bottom line, I know enough to get us out of here."

Sara chose not to press the matter. Splashing where Caesar was feeding made her take her eyes off the screen. It was a violent buffet, reminding her of the fate she and her friends would suffer if they failed to escape.

"Whoa!" Richard pointed at the screen. "You see that? What the hell was that?"

Sara turned her eyes back to the monitor. All she saw was blue water and rock fragments surrounding the shuttle.

"I didn't see anything."

"To the left," Richard said. "It went that way and… what the—" There was a blur of movement. Right then, the screen went fuzzy.

Sara tried steering it back. The red light at the top was now blinking, meaning the signal was not reaching its destination.

"It's dead."

"I thought those crabs couldn't swim," Richard said.

"Assuming something grabbed it, I don't think it was a crab."

"You can't steer it back?" Richard said. Sara shook her head. "So… we lost the drone?" Sara didn't offer a response, for the answer was obvious and enraging. Richard read between the lines. He took a moment to pace. Every cell in his body wanted to freak out in a delinquent rage. Just moments ago, he was looking at a possible way off of this planet, and their main tool to retrieve it was suddenly taken by God-knows-what.

He watched the horizon that stretched across that infinite blue. Even after everything he had been through, it was still an oddly beautiful sight. In a sense, it was hard to blame the entire ocean for the actions of a pack of ravenous crustaceans. Maybe on one of the other islands, it really was paradise. Maybe everything that happened was Challenger's way of telling Mankind to keep his dirty mitts off this planet.

"You've been here for months before there was any real sign of danger, yes?" he said.

"That's right," Sara said.

"I imagine you took time to swim."

Sara immediately knew what he was getting at. "Swimming. Diving. You can bet I've done it all."

"Does Dr. Kern or any of the others have diving gear?" Richard asked.

"If you're asking 'is there any gear that'll fit me?', yes there is," Sara said. "You remember how to dive?"

"Had training back on Earth," Richard said. "In murkier waters than this. I think I'll be fine."

Sara picked up the module and stood up. "Just so we're on the same page, you're planning to go down there and plant the lifting bags manually, yes?"

"That's right," he said.

"And if the shuttle's damaged?"

"We'll bring Dante with us to give it a look." With that said, Richard turned around and started walking to the station.

Sara jogged to catch up. "Listen, it's fairly deep around there. Forty-plus feet. There's something I have that'll help. We have diver propulsion vehicles in the maintenance shed that were left undamaged. We can use those during the dive."

Richard stopped. "We?"

"Gonna object?"

"We don't know what's swimming down there."

"We know what's splashing around out there." Sara pointed to the east shore where Caesar was feeding.

Richard gave the ocean a glance, then nodded reluctantly. "Don't blame me if some big... I don't know, crayfish pinches your ass while we're down there."

Sara winced at that thought. "First of all, crayfish are freshwater crustaceans."

"Maybe not the alien ones," Richard said.

"Fair enough." She followed him back to the station. "You're gonna sneak up on me and pinch me while we're down there, aren't you?"

CHAPTER 13

Jac watched Dante gather up his tools and scanning devices. Standing in front of the tower was Richard and Milla, the latter carrying two power cells in her pack.

"So, this is the plan?" he said. "Take our only engineer on a suicide mission? For what? Raise a dead shuttle?"

The words 'suicide mission' brought Dante to a halt. The engineer had a worrisome look on his face. He was already unenthusiastic about heading across the island to begin with. Jac's words only worsened the anxiety brewing within him.

He looked to the Corporal, hoping the man would come to his senses. It stood to reason their best bet was to fix the tower. Seeing the Corporal and Sara in their diving gear, it did not appear his hopes would be answered.

Richard tightened his jaw, refraining from a few unprofessional retorts.

"If this works, we can be out of here within the hour," he said.

"If it works… if you even survive," Jac replied. "*If* Dante dies, we'll have a hell of a time getting this tower back online."

The engineer leaned forward, his face paling at the mention of 'die'.

"The island might not last that long," Richard said.

"According to you," Jac said. "It's been breaking apart for days. If you ask me, we have more than enough time."

Richard wrinkled his nose. "Well, Jac, I didn't ask you. So, shut the fuck up. This is my call. You and Foreman will remain here and protect Drs. Kern and Cross. That is an order." He looked to Dante. "You set to go?"

Dante barely nodded. "You… uh, you sure this'll work, Corporal?"

Richard read between the lines. The real statement was *'If this plan is likely to get us out of here faster, then I'll do it.'*

"We saw the ship on the monitor," Richard said. "It's intact. We just need to get down there and raise it."

"You still didn't say what happened to the drone," Dante said.

Sara and Richard looked at each other, then back at him.

"We're not exactly sure."

Dante swallowed. "Well... that's comforting."

He joined Sara, who stood beside her supply droid. Essentially a supply cart on four legs, it was able to get around the uneven terrain with ease. Inside were the diver propulsion vehicles, the lift bags, an underwater flare pistol and cartridges.

"Ready to go," Sara said.

Dante gave the crane a quick lookover. Its frame was partly charred by the fire, but the mechanics were still functional.

"Ready to go," he confirmed.

The four of them turned south and started the short, but tense journey to the south ridge.

***

It had been a silent walk to the south end, with no presence except for a heavy dread that weighed on the four team members. Upon arrival on what was now the shoreline, or more accurately described as a miniature cliff edge, they took a minute to take in the view. The water lapped against the rubble where the cliff met the ocean. Farther out, the rest of the south shore's destruction was visible under the clear blue water. Somewhere in that broken landmass was their way out of here.

Richard checked his rebreather. It was a larger model than what they used in the Corps, and more awkward to have around his face. Not only that, but it only supplied two-thirds as much oxygen. Still, it would suffice for their needs.

He put the rebreather mask over his head and took a breath. Looking through the dome-shaped glass, he turned to face Sara. She already had hers on and was peering out over the cliff. It was a short three-foot drop into the water, nothing too scary.

On the ground next to her were their diver propulsion vehicles, simply referred to by researchers as DPVs. Their batteries were fully charged, the propellers and controls tested.

Their function was easy. Throttle forward, throttle back, twist the handle for increased speed.

Dante extended each of them an underwater supply bag to be strapped over their shoulders. Inside were three lift bags, attached to a magnetic connector device. The bags were large and heavy, each one designed for lifting sunken vehicles weighing several tons.

"You sure you can handle all of these at once?" he asked in a shaky voice.

"We'll be fine," Richard said. "Be ready with that cable and winch. We'll have to pull the ship close once we bring it up."

Dante nodded and backed up toward the machine.

Two yards left of him was Milla, standing ready with her Hunter Killer rifle in hand. She chuckled at the sight of Richard in his swim gear.

"What?" he asked.

"I can tell it's been a while," she replied. She pointed to his right ear.

Sara approached him and tightened the valve on the three-inch tank on the right side of his mask. "That would've been bad. Not notice it during testing?"

"Guess I breathed in regular air," he said. "How's it look now?"

She gave the other side of his mask a quick lookover, then cleared him with a thumbs up. "You'll live."

"Or at least, I won't die by suffocation," Richard added. He looked to Milla, who nodded. Nothing needed to be said. She already knew her job: keep an eye out and shoot anything that has more than two legs.

He wished he had the same luxury. Instead of his rifle, he only had his flare pistol and a knife. In addition to those, he had a few underwater charges to destroy any heavy rocks pinning the shuttle. He hoped he would not have to use them, but then again, this day had not been rewarding hope so far.

Richard tested the comm unit on his mask. "Let's go, Doctor."

"Getting formal now?" Sara asked as she joined him at the cliff edge. Not bothering to answer the question, he lowered himself into the water and extended his DPV. Sara was right behind him. They dipped below the surface to check for any movement. So far, all they saw was ocean. The sun was kind to them, giving a clear view of the area. They gave a quick wave to Milla and Dante, then committed to the dive.

Surrounded by lukewarm water, they moved their feet up and down like aquatic mammals. Twenty feet down, Richard felt heavier. The surface above had a sparkly, heavenly quality to it. Just another example of the planet's deceptive façade of tranquility.

The DPVs did most of the work, allowing them to cruise slowly but steadily toward the ocean floor. The bags lifted, causing a little bit of drag, but not hindering the descent too badly.

Midway to the bottom, Richard froze. There was a glimmer of movement somewhere to his three o'clock. He switched off his DPV motor and pointed his flare pistol, sweeping the ocean with its muzzle.

Sara stopped, watching the nervous marine. Slowly, she approached him.

"You see something?" she asked through the comm.

"Something's out there," he said.

"What'd it look like?"

"Not sure. Only caught a glimpse... wait..." He turned a few degrees to the right, then shrieked as a pan-shaped fish darted past him. "Jesus!" He leaned back, bumping into Sara, who immediately started chuckling.

The fish was no larger than a saucepan. It had green scales, a tiny mouth used for eating vegetation, and eyes which appeared to be half the size of its body. It swam around the two alien creatures, then swam up to Richard. It tried picking at the ends of his flippers with its tiny mouth.

"Git!" He shook his foot, scaring the little fish off. Watching it disappear, he took a deep breath and lowered his flare pistol.

"Gonna be all right, Marine?"

"Not funny," he said.

"The situation we're in? No. That little fish mistaking you for seaweed? A little bit."

Richard waved her off. The woman had been battling overgrown sea creatures long enough to be a tad numb to it. A fact made obvious by her next statement.

"Sorry. Not trying to be insensitive. I guess this is my way of coping," she said.

"I suppose it's better than you losing your head," Richard said. "Figuratively or literally."

"There's that." She looked straight down, spotting the cockpit of the shuttle. "And there's *that*!"

"I see it," Richard said. They reactivated their DPVs and descended the rest of the distance.

As they had seen in the drone's monitor, the front section of the shuttle appeared to be intact. There were a few scrapes and grooves in the hull from the crashing of land all around it, but no breach.

Richard pulled one of his lift bags and planted it on the neck of the ship, pressing a green key on the top to activate the magnet. A moment later, the lift may as well have been attached to the shuttle. For good measure, Richard gave it a tug. It was on there for good, its bag dangling, ready to inflate at the press of a button.

They would need to attach the others first.

Sara attached one to the other side of the shuttle, then worked their way down. They met at the midsection and attached another set of lift bags. Easy enough. Now to place a pair on the engines...

...Which were completely covered with rocks.

Richard moved to the starboard engine, cursing as he looked for a spot to place the next lift bag. From afar, the shuttle looked as though it was protruding from a hillside. Hundreds of pounds of rock and sediment completely obstructed the stern side.

"Geez," Sara said. She moved some of the smaller rocks, then put her feet to a boulder. "I don't know if we'll be able to move this. These rocks weigh at least three hundred pounds. The shuttle might be pinned."

"We'll have to use the charges," Richard said.

"Near the engines?" Sara said. "Is that safe?"

"It is if we only use the smaller ones," Richard said. "Use them on the big boulders. It'll be enough to break them into smaller pieces. We'll be able to clear them after that."

Sara answered with an exasperated sigh. She wasn't thrilled with the plan, but knew he was right. Either they attempted this risky plan or gave up. The lift bags would not work for these things, and there was no place to secure the crane's cable to lift them away.

Richard removed an explosive charge from his belt and placed it on the top of a boulder. He bit his lip, begrudging the situation. This was usually a job for a replaceable underwater demolition drone.

"Alright, move back," he said.

Sara was way ahead of him. Shockwaves and vibrations traveled further and faster in water than in air. Even a small blast could leave them physically stunned, or even unconscious.

Richard armed the charge then reversed his DPV. In a few short seconds, he was a hundred feet away. The charge detonated, the boulder cracking into several fragments which fell freely from the starboard engine. The blast did more than Richard bargained for, its force knocking much of the other debris off of the hull.

The two divers returned to the shuttle and began brushing the remaining rock from the starboard hull.

"Oh." Sara's voice was sullen as she stared at a large crack near the ion ventilator. "Richard, this doesn't look good."

"We can get Dante to patch it," Richard said.

"That might not be enough," she said.

"It won't affect the pressurization of the ship," he said. "Come on. Let's blast these rocks off the port engine and get these lifts attached."

He swam to the opposite engine, smacking some of the smaller rocks off before positioning himself over another large boulder. He pulled another charge from his belt and extended it toward the boulder.

"Shit!"

The explosive slipped from his fingers, descending toward the seabed. Richard reached out to grab it, but missed.

"Having trouble there?" Sara said.

"Oh, hush." Richard went after the thing. "Start moving back, will ya."

"What about my lift bag?"

"Wait till we've cleared this shit off, then we'll finish the job," he said.

"Alright." Sara moved out to sea.

Richard could see the red, tablet-shaped charge contrasting against the bottom. He picked it up, planting his feet on the ground as he redirected his DPV skyward.

The sight of that weird, big-eyed fish made him do a double-take. It was a few meters to his ten o'clock, picking at something lodged in the seabed. He squinted, noticing a sparling reflection of sunlight that only glass could cause. Thrusting his DPV, he moved closer to it, spooking the little fish. It hovered several feet over the diver, believing to have lost its potential snack to the larger creature.

Not that it mattered. The fish had already learned that metal, wires, and glass that made up underwater maintenance drones were not edible.

The manta ray-shaped device had been split in two, its center crushed as though caught in a giant pair of pliers. The metal near the incision was bent inward, indicating it had been caught in a narrow but powerful grip.

His mind immediately went to the crab's pincers.

That doesn't make sense. The thing was several feet up. Unless those things can swim—and it doesn't seem like they can—something else must've done this.

In the blink of an eye, the fish darted at an amazing speed, resembling a shooting star as it disappeared over the hillside. Richard understood the basics of animal behavior to know when one was fleeing from a threat. Usually, threats to fish tended to be large predators.

Richard looked to the west, freezing as his mind grasped the sight of the thing sharing the ocean with them. It moved like a snake, appearing to slither through the water. Its body was between twenty and thirty feet in length, thin like a knife, the top and bottom edges thin and flexible. An eel.

What separated it from familiar species of eel, other than its immense size, were its head and jaws. Its mouth, extending nearly four feet from its eyes, resembled an eagle's beak.

It was moving with intention, straight towards Sara. Facing away from the creature, she had no idea it was coming up on her.

"Sara! Look out!" he shouted.

She turned around, immediately gasping as she saw the open jaws.

In the moment he had, Richard could only think of one thing. He pointed his flare pistol at the eel and fired. A burning hot ball of fire spat from its muzzle, zipping between the eel and Sara.

The creature shut its jaws and veered to its right, surprised and irritated by the flickering red light. It followed the thing for a moment before losing interest and pointing its head back at Sara.

In her shock, she had lost the grip on her DPV. The bag weighed her down, making backpedaling difficult.

"Richard! Help!"

He extended his DPV in her direction and twisted the handle. The tactic nearly proved to be a mistake, for the striking speed at which it took off nearly caused him to lose his grip. Machine and marine took off like a rocket at sixty miles-per-hour.

Richard turned to the right, pointing it to the side of the creature's head.

Crash!

The impact knocked the creature to the right. It darted out to sea, clicking its jaws as its senses returned. It was probably unused to such impacts, judging by its sluggishness.

Neither was the DPV, apparently. Its engine was grinding, the front end split open.

"Sara, can you get to yours?" he asked.

"Yeah," she said. She fixed her posture and let herself sink to the bottom where her vehicle had landed. Looking up, she saw Richard was still stationary, roughly ten feet under the surface. The eel was not looking in his direction, its wriggly bodily motions launching it for another strike. "Rich! Get away!"

He thrust the damaged vehicle toward the predator, then spun out of the way. The eel bit down on the device and swam off, believing it to have caught a meal. In just a few short moments, it realized this thing it had bitten was just like the drone it had mistaken for a fish. Solid. Fleshless. Useless.

Unlike the drone, this mechanical victim carried a second surprise. The creature had no idea the human had planted an explosive charge in the crack of the device. Right after the eel tossed the DPV to the side, the charge detonated.

Caught in a shockwave, the eel twisted and turned, slowly falling toward the bottom. It was strangely graceful in the way it fell, its tailfin and mouth reaching for the heavens as though begging for salvation.

That angelic pose then twisted into a demonic form. The angry eel jerked its head back and forth, its beak ready to snap at anything that moved. Its senses were still warped from the shockwave. At this point, it was ready and willing to attack everything and anything.

Richard loaded a fresh cannister into his flare pistol and took careful aim. He needed to make sure the flare would be seen by the eel, yet lead it to deeper waters. *Away* from them.

He squeezed the trigger, launching the ball of flame in a near perfect arch. The eel spotted the red light, snapped its jaws and missed, then pursued the flickering target.

The hum of a DPV made Richard look down. Sara came up beside him, watching the creature disappear into the distance.

"Nice work." A shaky laugh followed the compliment. "Gosh, we've been back together for, what, an hour or two, and already you've saved my life twice."

"The hell was that thing?" Richard said.

"Hawk eel, and a big one at that," she said. "We've seen them around here before. They're fascinating but, as you saw here, mean."

"Then let's wrap this mission up," Richard said. He grabbed ahold of Sara's DPV and let her throttle them back to the shuttle.

Immediately upon arrival, Richard planted another charge on the rock, activated it, and let Sara steer them clear of the blast.

"Wonder what's going on down there," Milla said. "That last blast was nowhere near the shuttle. They shot off two flares."

"Maybe they've encountered the crabs," Dante said.

BOOM!

That latest blast was near the designated spot. What she knew for sure was that Richard was still alive.

"Gosh, I hope those charges aren't damaging the engines," Dante said.

"He'd only use it if there was something large pinning the ship down," Milla said.

"Doesn't change the risks," Dante said. "I'm good, but I can't fix an Ion engine with a few hand tools."

"Just keep calm. Everything's gonna be fine," she said.

The words had barely left her mouth before the planet chimed. The water thrashed, the tectonic plates beneath it grinding against each other with crushing force.

Milla and Dante both felt their blood pressure spike as the ground beneath their feet shifted violently. In that moment, there was a thunderous crunching sound somewhere behind them.

The seismic episode eased into a mild tremor. Milla and Dante stood frozen, both feeling as though the slightest movement might make the island break apart.

Dante swallowed, then shot a glare at Milla. "You were saying?"

Milla exhaled slowly, then glanced at their surroundings. She wasn't sure if it was her imagination, but she could swear she heard something moving somewhere inland. Her mind conjured up images of ravenous crustaceans slowly converging on them, eager to feed on their entrails.

She placed the two power cells strategically on the ground. All they needed was a well-placed plasma bolt, and the core would spark and spew its toxic fumes.

From then on, her time was spent watching the island and the water.

"Hurry it up, guys."

When Richard and Sara felt the quake, they initially thought they were too close to the detonation and were experiencing a shockwave. Feeling the shifting of water and the loose sediment below, they quickly realized the planet was continuing its agenda of rearranging the landscape.

For a moment, they spotted the eel in the distance. It still appeared frantic, either from the previous blast or from the earthquake. Fortunately, it did not notice them as it moved westward.

"We need to hurry up," Sara said. "They're territorial. It'll be back shortly."

With that in mind, they let the DPV bring them back to the shuttle. Richard immediately planted himself onto the port engine. The blast had successfully knocked away the heavier rocks. Like with the starboard engine, there was damage to the hull. It was something he would worry about later. Right now, he needed to worry about getting the thing to the surface.

He placed the lift bag on the hull, then turned to Sara. She gave him her last remaining lift bag, which he quickly planted onto the starboard engine.

Together, they swam to the surface.

Milla and Dante were on the shore, visibly nervous after the earthquake. Milla pointed to him, telling the engineer she had spotted the divers.

"Took you guys long enough!" she shouted.

Richard lifted his mask. "Had an issue. Tell you about it later. Dante, go ahead and activate the lifts."

The engineer eagerly picked up the detonator, linked it with the six units below, and initiated the inflation process.

Down below, the six cannisters filled their bags with air. The ultra-strong airtight fabric expanded, their combined strength successfully lifting the shuttle from the seabed. Clouds of sediment billowed as the spacecraft departed, bits of rock falling from its engines.

All at once, the red bags appeared on the ocean's surface, the outline of the vessel directly below them.

Having bolted the crane to the ground, Dante lowered the cable to the water. With no drone to take its clip to the shuttle, there was no choice but to have Richard take it over by hand.

He and Sara returned to the shore, the latter climbing out of the water. Richard took the end of the cable and turned around, using the DPV to take him back to the shuttle. He attached the cable to a cleat on the top of the hull, then returned to shore.

"Okay, Dante. You're up," he said.

The engineer stood by the instrument panel at the back of the machine. With a pull of a lever, he retracted the cable.

The four of them watched in silence and anticipation as the shuttle was gently pulled closer to shore. A feeling of reprieve began to come over them after seeing its steel hull through the rippling water. Just being near a starship was enough to energize their spirits. Optimism bias filled their minds, each person refusing to consider the likelihood of the ship not being operational. It needed to be functional. It *had* to be. Their very lives depended on it.

Dante extended the arm of the crane to its maximum length, its end twenty feet from the shoreline. He lifted the main hoist, bringing the shuttle over the water's surface.

"Hold it there," Richard said. He yanked off his flippers then hopped onto the shuttle, relishing the feeling of steel under his feet. "Get your ass over here, Dante. Bring your toys. The faster you move, the faster we can get out of here."

Dante picked up his scanner and stepped atop the shuttle. He leaned forward and back, the motion of the ship bobbing in the water threatening to throw him into the water. Richard grabbed a fistful of his shirt, stabilizing him.

"You all right?"

"Yeah," the nervous engineer said. He nodded and smiled to feign confidence. "Yeah! I'm... good." He carefully made his way to the port engine, kneeling by one of the gorges in its hull. In the blink of an eye, that fake smile turned into a very genuine frown. "Oh, this isn't good."

Those words brought the group's optimism bias to a crashing end. Milla stuffed a fresh cigar into her mouth and lit its end. Normally a pastime habit, it now served as a much-needed stress reliever.

"Not good?" she said. "Exactly *how* not good? Like... you might need an hour or two to fix it... or..."

"Or..." Dante's voice trailed off. He hoped his tone would convey the message. Seeing the look on the Corporal's face, he realized he needed to be blunt. "I think the ion shielding has been breached. Let me conduct the scan..." He placed the scanner over the breach and initiated the scanning sequence. Several digits scrolled over the small rectangular monitor, displaying codes that only a man of Dante's expertise would understand.

"Anything?" Richard asked.

Dante pursed his lips and shook his head. "Sorry, Corporal. There's too much interior damage. Water made its way through the covering. The plasma injectors are damaged, the exhaust neutralizer grid fried. The only way to fix it is to get new parts."

Richard turned around, on the verge of losing his mind. He stepped away from the engineer, whom he knew was feeling as defeated as he was. On shore, Milla and Sara stood silent, the former taking many long draws of her cigar. The Corporal watched the little clouds of smoke rise and disappear, becoming part of the planet's atmosphere. His gaze continued rising until it was focused on the sky and the dark void beyond it. Never in his life did he think he would prefer the dullness of that void over the gorgeous ocean scenery, but at least the blackness of space was predictable. Nor did it house any killer sea creatures.

Here he was, standing atop the only starship on the planet, and yet it may as well have been a million miles away. It was no more useful than a pile of scrap in a junkyard. This mission had been a big waste of time—time that could have been spent repairing the radio tower. Now, it would take even longer to fix that stupid unit, and in consequence, longer for the rescue team to arrive.

Big surprise. Jac was right. Should've just stayed at the station and waited for them to get a radio signal out...

"Radio..." he said aloud.

"Hmm?" Dante looked at him. A lightbulb went off in his mind, making him realize what Richard was thinking. Both men pointed to each other, their hearts rushing with newfound optimism.

Maybe, just maybe, the shuttle's radio was operational.

"Can you get into the cockpit from up here?" Richard said.

"Yeah! There's a maintenance hatch up this way." Dante grabbed his stuff and rushed past the marine. He found the hatch cover and slid it down, revealing the hatch door. He turned the wheel, unlatching it. The hinges creaked loudly as the hatch opened outward.

The engineer moved down the ladder into the shuttle's passenger area. From there, he made his way to the cockpit. Richard was right behind him. The interior was dark and foreboding, the only light shining through the open hatch. The cockpit was brighter thanks to the viewing glass, which allowed the sun's rays to grace the instrument panel for the first time in days.

Dante took a seat in the pilot's chair and plugged his scanner into the ship's computer. He raised both hands in the air as the scan results came back.

"Yes! There's enough residual power," he said. "Let me start up the computer system and I can get a message out."

Richard leaned against the bulkhead and shut his eyes. He felt fifty pounds lighter. Though he would rather be flying out on this ship right now, being able to make a call on its radio still saved them a lot of time. The freighter would get the signal and awaken a crew right away. It beat spending hours getting the island's tower operational.

The computer system came on. Up until now, Richard and Dante never appreciated the basic illumination of a ship's instrument panel. Dante directed the power to the ship's antennae for maximum signal boost.

He turned to the radio station. "Alright, here goes nothing..."

Had it been any other occasion, Sara and Milla would have spent their time chatting about life. They had known each other back on Rosseni and shared a few drinks. Things got a little awkward after the incident at the ridge, a feeling Milla still experienced. Sara seemed to be doing well, considering who she lost during that event. Perhaps being in this supposed paradise, before it turned to blue hell, helped her out.

"At first, he didn't want to come down here," Milla finally said. "Didn't think he'd be able to face seeing you again. Then we saw what had happened, and all of a sudden, he was willing to rip the island apart himself to find you. He went to check on that maintenance boat, even though the rest of us were like 'nah, don't bother.'"

Sara smiled. "No complaints here."

"I know I'm stating the obvious, but he's sorry," Milla said.

"I know he is," Sara said. "And he shouldn't be. It was a crappy situation. A call had to be made, and fast. Looking back, I can't say I know for sure that I would have made the right decision either."

Milla nodded. She remembered, having been there.

Their reminiscence came to a swift end as the sound of scurrying legs brought their attention to the northeast.

Both women shouldered their rifles, both exclaiming "Shit!" at the sight of several of those insectoid crustaceans approaching them. Like a colony of ants, they converged on the fresh meat at the shoreline.

"Can't catch a break, can we," Milla said. Clenching that cigar between her teeth, she fired the first shot. The target reeled backward, its thin shell cratering as the plasma bolt made explosive contact.

Sara shot next. A little rusty, her first couple of rounds went high. Remembering the training Richard had put her through, she leveled the barrel, centered the target in the iron sights, and landed her third shot.

The other creatures continued coming. Spurred by intense hunger, they held little fear for these alien weapons. All that mattered were the meat figures that wielded them.

Milla put a couple more down, then shook her head. "This is just great. There's more coming."

Sara landed another shot, then turned to face the shuttle. "Hurry it up, guys! We've got problems out here!"

Richard and Dante perked up at the sound of rifle fire and shouting.

"The hell's going on out there?" Dante said. They both looked to the viewing port on the lefthand side. "Uh-oh!"

"Son of a bitch." Richard went for the fuselage, stopping briefly at the cockpit entrance. "How much time do you need?"

"Radio station's powering up," Dante said. "Ship took a beating on the way down. Computer's a little sluggish. I'll make it work. Trust me."

That was good enough for Richard. He made his way to the maintenance hatch, reemerging on top of the vessel. Up on shore were several of those four-foot mantids. He hopped on shore and took part in the action, taking down multiple crustaceans with great speed and precision.

Hot blue bolts of energy struck shell, producing a stench of charred meat and calcium. Even with many of their members dead, the creatures kept coming.

"Gosh, were these things a problem before now?" Richard said to Sara.

"No," she said. "I think the series of earthquakes have interrupted the migration and feeding patterns of many different species, including the crabs. Where's Dante?"

"Trying to get the radio working," Richard said. He blasted another crustacean.

No matter how many of them they killed, their numbers never seemed to dwindle. For every one they killed, two more showed up. The agony of starvation was a powerful force, propelling the swarm toward the humans with no thought to the devastating force of their weapons. They feared nothing.

Almost nothing.

All at once, they stopped. They held their position, their upper bodies raised, the antennae on their heads waving.

The humans ceased fire, conserving their dwindling ammo, while also trying to figure out what was now going on.

In one collective motion, the swarm turned east and retreated to the sea. As soon as they disappeared, the sound of wedge-shaped feet chiseling on the island became loud and clear.

Richard looked to the west. Looking back at him were the big black eyes of two crabs. Cliff and Klin, the duo that always hunted together.

Milla spat out her cigar. "Corporal?"

"Yeah, I see them," Richard said.

"Probably heard the gunfire and vibration we caused while raising the shuttle," Sara said.

"What are we gonna do? These guns are worthless," Milla said. Already, the crabs began their approach. Milla, following her instincts, hit both of them with a barrage of blaster fire, proving her point.

Richard looked back to the shuttle, hoping to see Dante rising from the hatch. He was still in the cockpit, his figure visible through the viewing port. It was unclear what was going on in there, but it appeared he was frantically working on some controls. Maybe there was a malfunction. Perhaps he needed to find some extra power from somewhere. Whatever the reason was, he was moving frantically in the cockpit.

"CORPORAL?!" Milla shouted.

Richard knew there was no other choice.

"Throw the cells. Blast 'em."

Milla and Sara each took one of the cells and chucked them toward the crabs. No sooner did the cells hit the ground were they bombarded with blaster fire, which ruptured the protective casing, igniting the fluid inside. The twin explosions sent ripples through the shoreline and little pebbles flying through the air.

Hot plumes of chemical smoke burst from the flames, halting the crabs in their tracks. Cliff and Klin backed away, snapping their pincers at the expanding cloud. They backed away, their eyes still fixed on the delicious humans on the other side of that smoke tower.

A new disturbance brought the crabs to a halt. The ground came alive. With a mighty *crunch*, the shelf began to split.

Sensing the shift in several tons of rock, the two crabs turned around and scurried westward, disappearing as quickly as they arrived.

Richard, Milla, and Sara suddenly felt weightless. The shoreline was tilting into the water and moving away from the rest of the island.

"Go! Go! Go!" Richard said, pointing northward. Sara and Milla picked up whatever supplies they could and sprinted. After thirty yards, they came to the newly formed ravine where the island was splitting. They made bounding leaps, barely making it to the other side.

Richard waited for the other two to make it to safety, then looked back to the crane and shuttle. Dante was *still* inside.

"Damn it." He tossed his rifle to Milla and sprinted back to the shore. Midway back, the section of land shifted farther, colliding with the shuttle. The crane detached and fell over, striking the top of the shuttle. With the lift bags deflated and no crane to hold it up, the shuttle fell straight down.

As Richard neared what used to be the shore, he could see the water pouring into the open hatch. He pulled his mask over his face and dove straight down.

Surrounded by chunks of landmass, he followed the shuttle to the seabed. As he closed within ten feet, he was swept away by a gust of water and a cloud of silt. The shelf came apart as though struck by a demolition team, its chunks raining down atop the shuttle.

It had to have been entirely flooded by now, the person inside minutes from suffocation. Richard fought against the current, searching for the ship through the haze of sediment.

Unsuccessful in finding it near the pile of rock, he turned his eyes south.

There it was, the grey metal body of the shuttle. The big machine had been pushed over sixty feet to the south by the shockwave. Its cockpit, previously thought to be their salvation, now served as a death chamber for the man inside. The viewing glass was surprisingly intact, having been missed by the enormous rock fragments. A couple of boulders settled nearby, one of them resting directly in front of the nose.

Sucking in air through his rebreather, Richard zeroed in on the hatch. He entered the ship, now finding it completely dark, the corridors now home to thousands of gallons of salt water.

Thumping and muffled shouting echoed from the cockpit area. Richard swam through the corridor to the front of the ship, finding Dante, confused, panicked, and running out of air, pounding against the viewing glass.

Richard grabbed him by the shoulder and turned him around. Dante's mouth was open, the guy having spent the air in his lungs in a fit of panic. Richard smacked him on the jaw to calm him down, then pulled off his mask to slip onto the engineer's face.

Once the water was syphoned out, Dante took a few deep breaths. His lungs now filled with fresh oxygen, he began to calm down. Richard let the mask stay on long enough to point out his plans. He pointed his thumb behind him at the corridor, then up, signifying their escape through the hatch.

Dante nodded and gave a thumbs up. *I understand.* He took one more deep breath, then handed the mask back to Richard.

The marine put it on, allowed the water to siphon out from the inside, then took a breath. With the seawater gone, his vision was clear—allowing him to see the large shape on the other side of the viewing glass. That shape raised its two pincers, and with two simultaneous strikes, shattered the glass.

Huge shards fell into the cockpit, the barrier between the men and the open ocean gone.

The next thing Richard saw was Dante arching backwards, his freshly inhaled air bursting from his mouth with a large red cloud of blood. From his chest came the tip of Lance's lower left claw. The crab lifted its prize from the cockpit, the engineer grabbing at the pincer tip as though to somehow pry himself free.

The right claw shut over his right shoulder, then pulled. Another blood cloud left his mouth, his final moment filled with agony. A third, giant blood cloud filled the ocean as the crab ripped Dante's head and shoulders off the rest of him. Dangling the two parts from its claws, the crab pointed its eyes at the second human who watched dumbfounded in the ship.

Richard's mind reeled, contemplating the reality of Dante's sudden demise, while putting together the events that led up to it. That damn 'rock' that was in front of the ship was this damn crab. It had probably been sneaking for an ambush on shore, only to get thrown farther out to sea when the shelf collapsed. Either way, it still managed to snag a victim. Two, if it managed to get its claws on him.

It tossed Dante's parts aside, intending to do exactly that.

Richard backstroked, his left shoulder hitting the edge of the doorway. Somehow, probably due to the current rushing from forward and aft, or maybe from his own adrenaline, he found himself oddly stuck in this one spot.

The crab entered the cockpit and extended its good claw toward his neck. It was as though the big crustacean remembered him from when it had killed Walker, and was pleased to add Richard to its list of victims.

He reached for his pouch. If he was going to die, he would at least go out on his own terms. To his dismay, there were no more charges in the pouch. He was defenseless, with no gun, no explosives, not even a knife. All he had was that stupid flare pistol.

Richard shrugged and pointed the flare pistol at the crab. A squeeze of the trigger put a fiery ball right into Lance's right eye. Heat and blindness put the crab into a sudden frenzy. It scurried backward, out of the cockpit, onto the seabed. Watching the glistening red strobes, an idea came to Richard.

He loaded his final cartridge and fired the flare, landing it against the crab's carapace. The ball of flame stuck to the creature's hide as though it was coated with an adhesive. The beast hardly seemed to notice, for it was focused on the irritating sensation in its eye.

The first flare died out, the crustacean's frantic movements coming to an end. Paying no attention to the second flare burning against its side, the crab faced Richard again, raising its claws to finish what it had started.

It took a few steps in his direction, then stopped. In one swift motion, it turned left, a dark, narrow shadow coming over it from the south.

Richard looked high. To his slight surprise, the plan had worked. The big eel, still agitated from the previous events—and probably more so following the breaking of the island—shot right for Lance.

Like a rattlesnake striking a rodent, it lashed, slamming its jaws over Lance's left arm. The crab kicked its legs, its body spinning as the larger creature began pulling and twisting. Lance reached with its other claw, lacking the flexibility to reach the eel's bony jaws.

Its long body thrashed, the crab's fluttering limbs in the middle of this strange haze of fires and sediment.

A loud *crack* resounded from the middle of the chaos. The eel raised its head, carrying Lance's severed arm in its jaws. That shell, capable of withstanding energy projectiles and grenades, was no match for the hawk eel's crushing bite power.

Lance scurried backward, green blood spewing from the gap in its shoulder. The eel spat the limb and returned for another round. Lance snapped his good claw, which only ended up inside the eel's mouth. The next crunch was slow and tedious, even managing to make Richard squirm. Green blood spewed from the imploded claw.

Its shell as useful as cardboard against this enemy, Lance backpedaled. It was a sight Richard never thought he'd ever see: one of these giant crabs in full retreat. In fear.

The effort was futile. The eel grabbed the crab by one of its hind legs and yanked upward, flipping it onto its back. Pointed feet kicked upward, doing little to faze the eel as it went for the relatively softer underbelly.

Richard heard another *crunch* preceding the surgical opening of Lance's belly. Large flaps of shell opened up, exposing the soft juicy meat inside. The eel had no empathy for the fact its victim was still alive. All that mattered was consuming the delicious crab dinner. If the meal was still kicking, that was its problem as far as the meal was concerned.

It was a bittersweet moment for Richard. On the one hand, it gave him satisfaction to watch Lance meet a painful end. On the other hand, it didn't change anything. It killed Walker and it had killed Dante. Worse yet, there was no way of knowing if Dante had gotten a radio call out. Without him and the crane, repairing the communications tower would be damn near impossible.

The satisfaction from witnessing Lance's death shriveled as guilt took over. Dante didn't even want to come over here. He had initially agreed with Jac. Now he was dead, and Richard was now faced with the question of whether it was his fault.

It was a question that would have to wait. For now, he needed to regroup with the others and return to Smith Station, where a furious Jac would await them.

CHAPTER 14

"What happened? Where's Dante?"

Jac was near the maintenance shed, his face rigid after counting only three people in the returning group. Foreman was near the station entrance with John Kern and Ben Cross, all of whom eagerly awaited to hear the results of the mission.

Seeing the sullen, deflated expressions on Richard, Milla, and Sara's faces cast a dark shadow over the group.

Richard attempted to walk by Jac without saying anything, leading to him being stopped by a hand to the shoulder.

"Corporal? What. Happened?"

"Dante's dead," Richard said, brushing Jac's hand away. "The shuttle's destroyed. Another section of island broke it away."

"The hell you mean he's dead?!" Foreman said. "What the hell happened over there?"

"We brought the shuttle out of the water," Richard said. "The engines were too badly damaged for transport…"

"As I told you they would probably be," Jac said.

"…*but*… We thought there was enough residual power to use the shuttle's radio to get a signal out. Dante went inside, got everything working…" Richard's voice trailed off, furthering Jac's frustration.

"And? What? Did he get a call out?"

"I don't know," Richard said. "I had to step out. We ran into some trouble. The crabs showed up. We had to use the two cells to fend them off, or else we would have been screwed. Then another quake happened and the shelf broke off. Took the shuttle down into the water. I tried to get Dante out, but one of the crabs beat me to him."

Jac backed up, his pupils narrowing, the skin on his face twitching. Had it been just the two of them on this planet, he may have lifted his rifle muzzle and given the Corporal what he thought he deserved.

"Getting more people killed, huh?" Jac said. "I warned you that would happen."

"The plan almost worked," Richard said. "We had the shuttle…"

Jac scoffed. "Which was busted to begin with."

"Dante was going to get a call out…"

"Did he?" Jac said. Richard wanted to say yes but could not. Not with certainty, at least. He wasn't in the cockpit at the time. He couldn't know. All he did know was that it appeared Dante was having some kind of technical issue. That's how it appeared when he looked through the viewing port. The look on his face served as an answer for Jac's question. "Well, yippe-fucking-do. Good call, you big dummy."

"Just… Stow it, Private," Richard said.

"To hell with that," Jac said. "You think you can issue an order to shut me up? Your rank is meaningless to me now. Especially since it's gonna be stripped. Hopefully they put you in a brig for your idiocy. Had you just shut your mouth and kept Dante here, he'd be alive and we'd be well into the repair process."

"Where's the crane?" Foreman asked.

"Got lost when the shelf broke," Milla said.

The two marines looked simultaneously sick and on the verge of madness.

"So much for fixing the tower," Foreman said. "Well, we're absolutely, irrefutably screwed. Thanks, Carson. Glad you felt only getting one marine killed wasn't enough. Had to include the rest of us. Brilliant decision making."

"The hell you guys talking about?" Ben Cross said. "What happened? Did I miss something? He got someone killed?"

"A few someones," Foreman said. "Back on Rosseni."

"Leave it be," Richard said. "A decision had to be made. Both then, and now."

"And you made the wrong one both times," Jac said. He turned to the others, proudly willing to humiliate the Corporal by announcing his shortcomings and failures. "We spent two years on Rosseni. Dr. McQuade is well aware of the type of place that was. She and her brother, Martin, were in research. She was in marine biology and Martin was in geology. Rosseni, being a big heap of rock, was lacking in water, to say the least, but some researchers believed there to be water reserves on that planet.

"Well, within the settlements on that planet and neighboring worlds, an eco-terrorist group began to form. These idiots called themselves 'Liberators', as in environmental liberators, but eco-terrorists are what they really were. They wrecked a fuel rig on the north hemisphere hills, then decided to turn their sights on the McQuades' operation.

"See, they had successfully located an underwater lake, which would provide an adequate water source for the colonies if used properly. Of course, they needed to explore it first, test the water, see what's living in it, etcetera. Science stuff. They needed to construct a large drill, burrow down into the lake and gain access.

"Long story short, the so-called Liberators managed to gain access to weapons and some explosives. Somehow or another, they got wind of the fact that the researchers were going to explore the lake. Well, they didn't like that, so they attacked the drill site and held multiple workers and scientists hostage. Our team was dispatched, as we were the nearest squad available.

"We arrived on scene and met resistance. In that time, the Major in Hawthorne Base ordered a squadron of Hornets to execute a lightning strike on the base. For those who don't know what that is, essentially, they fire large cannisters that emit strong electrical particles, like EMPs, except they can also shut down a person's heart. Medical staff were on standby, so the rationale was to immediately tend to the hostages and revive them if necessary.

"Well, we realized the jackasses were trying to form a machine gun nest on the north side, which would have wreaked havoc on our incoming air support. Walker led some of us over to take it out. Richard and a couple guys remained on the south side to monitor the stronghold. Lo and behold, he comes to the conclusion they were intending to suicide bomb the place before the Hornets have a chance to sting 'em."

Richard pointed a finger. "Listen, man, they did the exact same thing on the cell freighter over on Maysi. Blew up a ship and themselves with it. They're fanaticals, Jac. Ideologs. They believe in the cause and value it over their own lives. That type of enemy is the most unpredictable and the most dangerous. They were setting up explosives all around the equipment, knowing full well the only other drills were fifteen-hundred miles away."

"So…" Jac continued, ignoring Richard. "He tries to sneak through the perimeter. To his credit, he managed to eliminate a couple scouts and disable two of the three set explosives before they got wind of him. Well, they saw him, and a firefight followed. Boom. They detonated the third charge. Two hostages and one marine died as a result. Not to mention some of the other injuries some of us left with that day."

He turned his cheek, revealing the remnants of scorch marks that even the med tanks could not heal.

"Of course, our colonel was a softie. One of those college types with hardly any field experience. Bought into the compassion nonsense, which is probably why he didn't have the balls to give this idiot any real punishment. Just assigned him to clerk duty until it was time to rotate back home."

Jac gestured at Sara. "His ex moved over here to get away from his sorry ass. I mean, who would want to date someone who got her brother killed? Am I right?"

"Jac." Sara's voice was soft, yet stern. The marine was ready to keep going, but managed to shut his jaw at the last second. He was bringing her loss into it now, which she did not appreciate.

He turned around and marched to the west side of the station. "Come on, Foreman. Let's walk perimeter."

"What about the tower?" Foreman asked.

"Unless you can lift it with your bare hands, the tower's a no-go. You're strong, but not that strong, big guy. We'll need to come up with something else. I think better when I'm walking." He looked over his shoulder. "Coming, Milla?"

She shook her head. "I'll stand watch up front."

"Suit yourself." With that said, Jac and Foreman began their patrol.

Richard quickly went for the station. "I'll be inside. Let me know if you see anything, Milla."

"What are you going to do, Corporal?" Milla said.

Richard turned around, hands out. "Get out of this wetsuit? Can I even make that decision without being questioned?!" He didn't expect an answer. He entered the station, found one of the crew quarters, ripped his diving suit off, and put his utilities back on.

His pants were barely on when someone knocked on the door.

"Not now, Sara," he said.

"Nah, it's me, Corporal." 'Me' turned out to be Dr. Ben Cross of all people. Richard opened the door, finding the medical doctor standing in the hall with a couple of beers in hand. "Wanna take a breather?"

Richard looked at the beers, then up at the doctor's face. "What is this? A 'one last drink before we die' sort of thing?"

Ben shrugged. "You can look at it that way."

An hour ago, Richard would have balked at such a mindset. Now, it seemed like just the thing to do.

"Fine."

The two of them walked into the lab and took a seat. Ben popped the caps off and slid one of the bottles over to Richard.

"Take a breather, Corporal," Ben said.

"Not much else to do," Richard said. "Even if we manage to find a way off this stupid island, there's no way to communicate with the outside."

"Maybe your engineer managed to contact the freighter."

"Maybe. Maybe not. Probably not. He would've gotten out the minute he was finished." Richard took a long drink. "The decision we face is, wait here and go down with the island, or construct a raft or something to paddle our asses across the ocean and set up camp on another landmass. Hopefully somewhere that isn't crawling with hungry crabs."

"Giving up?" Ben asked.

Richard almost chuckled. "Doc, last I checked, I can't snap my fingers and make a new starship appear. The boats are all wrecked. The nearest piece of land is hundreds of miles away. Yeah, I'm giving up. Why does that bother you? You seemed pretty content with giving up before."

Ben lifted his beer and smirked. "Yeah, I guess I've come so close to dying lately, I was ready for it to be over. Not like I have anything to look forward to anyway. Just another middle-of-nowhere assignment with a handful of other rejects."

"Sounds like my future," Richard said. "Who knows? Maybe we would've been stationed together. Could've gotten drunk on a nightly basis, compared our screw-ups. It's one of those what-could've-been moments."

Ben gave a downtrodden smile. He watched the fierceness in which the marine clutched his drink, as though it reminded him of something.

"There's no guarantee the other guy's plan would've worked, just so you know," he said.

Richard took another slug and put the bottle down hard against the table. "Trying to make me feel better, Doctor? I thought you were supposed to be my new drinking buddy. Not a therapist."

"Fair enough. It's just…" Ben's voice trailed off but his eyes remained on Richard's beer.

"What?" Richard lifted the bottle. "You want mine?"

"No," Ben said with a snigger. "It's just… the way you're drinking is the exact same way I started. Literally with the same rock-solid grip, as though you're trying to strangle the bottle as you're draining it." His grin slowly faded. "Listen, man. We all make calls in life that don't play out the way we thought. In our professions, it can result in death."

"Yeah, well… I let my heart do the talking back on Rosseni," Richard said. "Sara's brother, Martin, became a good buddy of mine. I saw those pricks hitting him with their guns while the other ones were getting ready to blow the place up. Yeah, I was certain they were going to suicide themselves, but I wasn't sure whether they could pull it off before the Hornets arrived. But seeing them do that… shit, man. I decided to go at it with my fireteam. Bang bang boom. Caused the very thing I was trying to prevent. Killed one of my men in the process." He scoffed, staring into the distance. "Just like Dante, Private Lowry didn't even want to follow me there. He thought the Major's plan was right, but you know, I ordered him and he followed me."

Ben eyed his drink, reminiscently.

"Wasn't any emotional connection in my case. I just liked working and was good at my job. Yeah, I had a few drinks, and I could've warned the medical center that I was a little tipsy. But, you know, I thought 'hey, I've got this'. Well, I found out the hard way that I didn't, and an innocent person paid the price." He pushed the beer away, suddenly put off by it. Maybe it was the way he saw his actions mirrored by Richard, or just the mere thought of his failure. "I think I'll go for a water instead."

"Wow. I guess my newfound hobby will be experienced alone, huh?" Richard said.

"Maybe your newfound hobby should be cutting yourself a little slack," Ben said. "Trust me, I know all about punishing yourself. We were both handed crappy situations, Corporal. Situations that didn't pan out for the best. Maybe it's time we learned to live with them."

Richard almost laughed at that. "Right. Sure."

"Hey man, at least you made a considerably reasonable judgment call," Ben said. "Me? I was drunk and egotistical. Invincible. Until I realized I wasn't."

Richard looked at the two beers. "Well, maybe we can forgive ourselves in the few hours we have left."

"Giving up, are we?" He looked to the hallway entrance as Sara stepped in. She looked at Ben, mildly surprised to see him holding a water bottle instead of a beer bottle. "Mind if I have a word with the Corporal?"

Ben gestured at the fridge. "Anything you want from here first?"

"No thanks."

He shut the fridge and passed her on his way into the hall. "I'll be up front. The pretty Russian marine lady looks like she could use some company."

"Glad to see you have your priorities straight," Sara said. She took a seat across from Richard, looking him in the eye as he polished off his beer bottle.

He wiped his face and glared at her. "What?"

"Don't do this, Richard," she said. "We need you at your sharpest."

Richard slid the bottle away and reached for Ben's abandoned drink. "Be sharp for what? You think I want to be sober when those crabs eat us? Or when we plunge into the ocean? Whichever is first."

"We don't know that."

"Don't know, Doctor. Looks to me like the island's coming apart faster and faster."

Sara reached over and pulled the beer from his hand. "First of all, call me by my damn name. Secondly, you know what I was referring to."

"Okay, *Sara*." Richard reached and defiantly retrieved his beer. "To your point, I think you ought to prepare for the worst. It's not likely anyone will come for us. This mission turned out to be nothing but false hope for you. Had it not been for us, it would already be over for you. Suffocating is no joke, but in my opinion, it beats being eaten."

Sara kept an unblinking gaze locked on him, debating whether or not to take the beer from him.

"You think Dante didn't get the call out?"

"I know he was scared as shit," Richard said. "I know he's dead because of me. Had I just shut the hell up, there'd at least be a chance of getting out of this mess. The guys would be fixing up the tower right now."

"I thought you didn't think the island would last long enough for that," Sara said.

"Better odds than getting your only engineer killed," Richard said. He lifted the bottle to his lips. "Jac's right. I should've kept my yap shut and let them do their thing. Going after that shuttle was a suicide run. It's a miracle the rest of us made it back alive."

"No, it's not," Sara said. "We knew what we were all getting into."

"You decided to follow my lead," Richard said. "I made the wrong call. Again. First, I got Martin killed. Now..." He looked Sara in the eye. *Now I've gotten you killed too.* He raised his beer to drain the remaining half.

Sara broke eye contact, running her finger across the table as she formulated what she wanted to say.

"It's not you who should be sorry," she said. "It's *I* who should be sorry."

The beer stopped short, slowly lowering back to the table while Richard gave her a look of bewilderment.

"Beg your pardon? Have you drained a few of these while I wasn't looking?"

She snickered. "No, Richard. Listen to me. What happened at Rosseni... I was wrong to blame you. Way wrong. It's astonishing, really. You didn't ambush Martin and my colleagues, beat them down, and use them as hostages. Those pricks did. You were forced to make a call."

"I wasn't forced. Nobody made me," Richard said. "It was my call. And mine alone."

"And for all we know, it was the right one," Sara said. "Those guys were happy to detonate the bomb they had already set up. As I reflect on it, I think you were right. They were planning on suiciding themselves with the rig. Had you not intervened, there would have been more bloodshed." She shut her eyes and leaned away from the table. "I wish I didn't leave you."

"Well..." Richard gestured at the window. "You would have anyway. Come on, you're a marine biologist on the ass end of the universe. Opportunities like this only come once in a while."

"I would have rather stayed with you."

A long silence came between them. Richard held the beer, his jaw clenched shut, his mind unable to find words.

"I missed you," she added. "Some things are better than career opportunities. Work comes and goes. But what we had... that only comes once in a lifetime."

He put the bottle on the table and pushed it away, his desire to drown his self-loathing in alcohol suddenly gone.

"You sure you're not just saying that because you've nearly been eaten by giant crabs?"

Sara laughed. "No, I promise." She extended her hand.

Richard reached across the table and clasped it. Another silence filled the room, for no words were needed for either of them to know what the other was thinking.

The crushing weight of guilt had vanished. Richard felt lighter, his mind clear. Motivation directed his thoughts toward the directive. That objective: stay alive and wait for pickup. God willing, Dante had gotten that call out in time.

He stood up and spoke into his radio. "All units, report to the front of the station."

CHAPTER 15

A game plan had been set. Jac and Foreman, much to Richard's relief, did not argue with the procedures he laid out. Neither of them were willing to acknowledge his command at the moment, but there was nothing in his instructions they disagreed with, so they went along with it.

It was simple; monitor the decay of the island. In the event of an emergency, retreat to the tower area, which had the highest elevation on the island. In the meantime, they would collect whatever scrap they could and weld patches over the last remaining boat. The motor wasn't working, having been damaged by crab claws, the explosion, and environmental exposure to the interior. Jac was handy with a welding torch, and patching up the boat was a better use of time than patrolling idly, waiting for the crabs to show up. It wasn't as though he would be able to fight them off with his weaponry, as his team had already learned the hard way.

As Jac handled the patching, Sara and Richard tried to fix the boat's radio. It was not designed for off-planet transmissions, but it was all they had. First, they needed to replace some of the wiring, for the console had been damaged by Boat One's explosion.

All the while, they kept a watchful eye on the water. Richard vividly remembered watching Caesar gorging in the shallows. A big crab carried a big appetite. Sooner or later, he would be back for more.

"Wonder where the big one is," Richard said.

"Probably clinging to the rock shelf," Sara said.

"Big crustaceans like that can climb?" Richard said.

Sara nodded. "They're like spiders. They're able to dig their feet in and climb steep heights. This island's practically standing on a mushroom stem. The only way they can make their way up here is to climb like spiders until they reach this so-called shallow area."

"Maybe he's full," Foreman said. "You said you saw him chowing on some calamari, right?"

"Yeah, but that doesn't mean much, it seems," Richard said. "These crabs need to eat their own weight almost daily it seems." He noticed Sara chuckling. "What?"

"Oh, nothing," she said.

"No. What?"

She shrugged. "Just... I always wondered if you paid attention whenever I yapped about sea life."

"Aww," Foreman said.

"Aww," Jac followed, his version a tad more condescending. Romance wasn't as cute when they were trapped on a planet with hungry sea monsters out to get them. "How's that radio?"

"Seems fixed, but I can't boost the signal," Richard said. "Unless there's a vessel right outside our atmosphere, nobody's gonna hear our calls."

Jac shook his head slightly and ground his teeth, suppressing a rant about how he and Dante could be working to fix the radio tower. Alas, the marine kept his mouth shut. He had spoken his piece when the group returned from the shuttle mission. Right now, he needed to focus on the situation at hand.

Even if he did want to say something, he would not have been able to. The sound of blaster fire made them all turn toward the station. Milla's machine gun was going off.

"Hey, fellas! We've got Abbot and Costello arriving from the west," Milla said through the radio.

The marines and Sara sprinted west. After several meters, they could see the flashing of plasma bolts. Upon arrival, they found the two crabs converging on the station, a mere thirty feet from Milla, who had her machine gun set up in front of the lounge area. The heavy blaster fire successfully slowed the crabs down and forced them to raise their claws over their eyes. With their pincers absorbing the punishment, they inched forward.

Milla glanced at her fellow marines. "Can't hold them off for all eternity."

"We'll need to use our remaining power cells," Richard said.

Milla hit Cliff, then panned her gun to the right to hit Klin with a barrage of blaster fire. "Figure something out quick, because the moment they get a break, they start speeding up."

Illustrating her point, Cliff picked up speed, forcing Milla to refocus her machine gun fire on him.

Richard tapped Foreman's shoulder, then pointed at the crabs. "Hit 'em."

Foreman sprinted a few steps, took aim with his grenade launcher, and blasted away at the big crustaceans. The blasts successfully flipped the two creatures on their backs. They were unharmed, their agitation demonstrated by the kicking of their legs and claws, but it bought Richard and Jac the time they needed to place the remaining cells.

The crabs righted themselves and faced the humans, who were now all grouped in front of the patched-up habitat. The blaster fire had stopped, making the assault easy. Or so they thought.

Richard and Jac waited, each one taking aim at one of the cells. As the crabs neared the barrier, the two marines popped off several shots.

The power cells erupted, blue fire sticking to the thunderstruck crabs. The toxic mist expanded, driving the crustaceans back. With their claws encased with some of the burning fluid, they spun in place. Living underwater, they were unused to the concept of fire. Quick bursts of heat from the humans' plasma rifles was one thing. Those little bolts of energy appeared and disappeared in the blink of an eye. But steady flame was new. Moreover, it produced an uncomfortable gas that irritated their vision, produced a dryness in their mouths, in addition to other symptoms.

Cliff and Klin backtracked, eventually disappearing behind the elevation in the island's interior. The marines stood ready, waiting for them to reappear.

After a few minutes, Ben Cross appeared between the gaps of the front lounge patches. "Are they gone?!"

"For now," Richard said.

John Kern emerged through the entryway, looking at the fumes. "Those were our last cells. Once those burn out, we won't have anything to keep those damn things back."

"We could barricade the station a little better," Milla said.

"Won't hold them off for more than a minute," Sara said.

"Neither will going head-to-head with them," Jac said. "Grenades can't even crack their shells. All we can do is finish prepping that boat and hope for the best."

"And if they come back before you're finished?" Ben said.

"Then we retreat to the docks," Jac said.

"Won't do much good if the hull still needs work," Milla said. "We'd just sink."

"In other words, we'll be trapped at the shore, and the crabs will eat us there instead of here," Ben said. "Fabulous gameplan."

"Don't see you pitching in, boozer," Jac retorted.

That exchange led to a chaotic melee of words between the group. Insults and ideas were traded back and forth, tones got harsher, voices got louder.

All the while, Richard Carson watched the smoke and the geography behind it. Those damn crabs had been hit with fumes numerous times, yet only sustained minimal damage.

Poison. It seemed to be the only tactic that affected the creatures.

His mind went to work, ignoring the tense arguing behind him. Everything was a guess at this point. All he could do was make the best one he could and go from there.

He didn't believe they would fix up the boat before the crabs returned. Holing up inside the station would only box themselves in. Retreating to the docks would only change the setting in which they would be devoured. The only way to survive the next hour would be to kill the crabs.

"Hey, Doc. Unless you're suggesting how to win at beer pong, shut your mouth," Jac said.

"Come on, guys," John said. "Knock it off."

"Is this seriously what we're doing?!" Sara said. "Wasting time arguing?!"

"No. We're not," Richard said. A much-appreciated silence eclipsed the group as they turned their eyes to the Corporal. "We're not gonna run and hide. We're gonna invite Cliff and Klin back for dinner."

"Yeah?" Jac said. "Your grand plan is to stand our ground? Exactly how many beers did you have with Dr. Cross?"

"We are going to stand our ground, and we're *not* going to fight them. At least, not in the way you're thinking," Richard said. He looked at Sara. "Those poison sacs from the cephalopod creature, what would it do to them?"

"If they ingested it?" Sara shrugged. "I can only speculate, since I haven't been able to study the crabs' internal physiology. That being said, it would cause blood poisoning, brain poisoning, confusion, possibly bouts of extreme aggression. Madness, if you will. Probably organ shut down. Maybe paralysis. Ultimately, death. Knowing them and their high metabolism, they would probably experience the effects pretty damn quickly."

Richard nodded. "That's probably an accurate assessment. After all, they know to avoid eating those sacs."

"You mean to trick them into consuming the poison," Sara said. It was a realization and not a question.

"If they know not to eat the sacs, how do we get them to ingest it?" Foreman said.

"We retrieve the sacs, extract the poison from them, then inject it into some bait," Richard said. "Sara, you have any suggestions on what those crabs will eat?"

"Pretty much anything," Sara replied. "I will say, they seem to prefer human flesh over any other options. They'll eat the mantids but will ignore them when more appealing prey is nearby. Obviously, they'll eat cephalopods, large fish, eels… invertebrates!"

"Invertebrates?" Milla said. "As in worms? Why does that have you so excited?"

Sara instructed the crowd to follow her into the station. They gathered near one of the large machines in the lab, which turned out to store several specimen bins. Sara slid one of them out, revealing what appeared to be a large earthworm. It was alive, its body in a tight coil. Stretched at full length, the creature would be at least a meter long.

"We've been collecting some of these worms for analysis," Sara said. "They extract a fluid which may hold the key for fighting several illnesses."

"How many do you have?" Richard said.

"Two."

"Will the crabs eat them?" Foreman asked.

"Only one way to find out." Richard slung his rifle over his shoulder and went for the exit. From there, he turned east to retrieve those poison sacs.

CHAPTER 16

The worms did not take kindly to being removed from their storage containers. Being aquatic animals, they preferred the sanctuary of seawater. Even if they were terrestrial, they still would not have appreciated being strapped onto one of the lab tables. Tethered from the head, tail, and midsection, they squirmed in place while the scientists assembled near the poison sacs, found and retrieved by Richard.

The rubbery outer casing was surprisingly thick. Ben used his portable X-ray scanner to pinpoint the poison contents. For Sara, it was an interesting study, for she never had an opportunity to examine the physical structure of these sacs. There were two layers of thick muscle for them to penetrate before they reached the storage point. Complicating the process further was the abundance of nerves in the sac. If one got triggered, it would expel the poison contents with explosive force. In a normal situation, they could salvage the spilled poison. However, they needed it fast and ready to inject into the bait.

This is where Ben Cross' expertise came in handy. Using his biopsy needle, and years of experience, he bypassed the nerves and extracted the poison. Using a second needle, he retrieved another sample from the next sac. Now, it was time to prep the bait.

It was with no pleasure that he injected the worms. Even in this circumstance, it felt like cruelty. Sara wasn't pleased with the circumstance either. She came here hoping to study these animals, not use them as sacrificial lambs. But ultimately, the worms' lifespan would be cut short. Once the island fully collapsed, the crabs would eventually dig through the rubble and find them.

Their writhing quickly reduced to a mild wriggle. The poison coursed through their circulatory system. Their incredible immune system kept them alive for the next few minutes, whereas most other creatures would already be dead. This made the worms the ultimate trap, for the crabs clearly preferred live prey.

Sara and Ben carried the worms outside. The power cells had stopped burning, the breeze having carried the fumes far away.

Milla stood firm at her machine gun mount, the muzzle pointed southwest at the elevation where Cliff and Klin retreated earlier.

"Hope you guys are ready, because I think I heard something over there," she said.

Richard, Jac, and Foreman formed a firing line, John Kern standing around the corner to make sure nothing snuck up on them from the north.

Sara and Ben placed the bait seventy feet from the station. Both froze, hearing the rustling of rocks on the other side of the hills. That crushing and scraping got nearer and more intense.

"Yep, our guests are back," Ben said.

The two of them backed away. Sure enough, Cliff and Klin emerged, their eye stalks angling at the two humans.

"Come on over," Sara said. "We've put out appetizers. Come and get 'em!"

The two crabs began making their way closer to the humans. They moved with caution, possibly concerned about another toxic cloud. They inched closer, claws extended, ready to both attack and defend their eyes from blaster fire.

Seventy feet in front of them, seven hearts were racing. All four marines took steady breaths in through their nostrils and out through their mouths. It was the best method for keeping calm in the wake of certain death. If this plan failed, they may as well turn their guns on themselves.

"This better work, Carson," Jac hissed.

"It will," Richard replied, his gaze never leaving the creatures. Behind them, Ben Cross was reaching for his flask. He was already reconsidering his decision to quit alcohol. John Kern was no longer watching the north, as Cliff and Klin's approach had his full attention.

The worms continued to wiggle, their slimy flesh creating a white and purple foam.

Richard squinted, noticing the oddity. He leaned over to Sara. "Is that normal?"

"For them to excrete? Yes," she said. "For the excretion to be that color? No."

"Son of a bitch," Jac muttered. "Their bodies are expelling the poison. The crabs might see it and ignore them."

"No," Richard said. "They only know to ignore the squid's poison sacs. They won't recognize the poison itself."

"You better be fucking right about that," Foreman muttered.

"Stand fast, damn it," Richard said. "It'll work. Everybody, hold your ground."

Jac and Foreman shared a glace, seeing the same tense look in each other's eyes. That look conveyed one thought: *Do we follow this asshole's lead or not?* With no other alternative, they held their ground.

The two crabs came within five feet of the worms. Their eye stalks were still high, the black gaze seemingly fixed on the humans. The speed of their approach did not waver. Together they marched.

Three feet. Two.

They were now passing over the worms.

"So much for your grand plan," Jac said. He took aim, ready to go out fighting.

The crabs stopped and backed away. Their eye stalks tilted downward to inspect the three-foot creatures wiggling on the ground. Cliff leaned forward, inspected the invertebrate, then immediately snatched it up. The excretion did not bother the crab at all. Like a big, thick spaghetti noddle, the worm was slurped up.

Klin went for the other worm, only to be pushed aside by the greedy Cliff, who grabbed the second worm and gulped it down. Klin inspected the surrounding ground in search of any other invertebrates.

"Cliff ate both of them," John said.

"Go figure," Foreman said in a low, growly voice. "The plan half-worked. Even if he bites the dust, that still leaves the other one."

"Wait," Milla said. She pointed at Cliff. "What's it doing?"

All eyes went to Cliff. A bubbly foam was forming at its mouth. It was white at first, then green, as though the crab was vomiting its own blood.

Klin came up behind him, still searching for any scraps. The claws scraped Cliff's rear. The crab spun around and attacked, catching his hunting partner by surprise. Both claws clamped on Klin's right arm and applied intense pressure. Klin tried backing away, but his attacker refused to let go. Every attempt to pull away was futile. Cliff had gone on the warpath, only instead of going after the delicious humans, he was going after his own kind.

"Someone's not happy," Ben muttered.

Richard smiled. "Like Sara said, consuming that poison can cause damage to the organs, including the brain."

"He's gone mad," Sara said.

Cliff pushed with intense force. There was no rhyme or reason for his violent actions, except that his insides felt as though they were on fire. The crab was not even hungry. His instinct-driven mind had gone haywire. With his nerves firing like never before, defensive reflexes kicked in. For these crabs, defensive tactics tended to be the same as offensive—kill anything nearby. The only difference was that it wasn't for hunger this time.

After backing away for several more steps, Klin finally had enough. It was time for his lifelong companion to either stop or bite the dust. He snapped his left claw, snagging the joint on one of Cliff's legs. The claw pressed tightly, cutting through the chitin.

SNAP!

The front half of the leg fell free. Cliff leaned to the right, the sudden pain and shift in weight loosening his grip. Klin managed to pull away free. The two crabs circled each other, claws open, poised to strike.

Normally, Cliff would have continued the standoff, searching for a weakness in his opponent. His basic ability to strategize was gone, however. His vision was now foggy, the sunlight now appearing green and red, the ground appearing to move all by itself. And in the middle of this vision was Klin, who held his claws in an aggressive stance.

Cliff sprang. Though clumsy and predictable, he still managed to catch his hunting partner off guard by his sheer ferocity. Fueled by madness, Cliff managed to sidestep Klin's guard and attack his right side. One claw secured a grip on a leg, the other stabbing at Klin's carapace. Bits of shell chipped away with each impact, forming the foundation for a large crack.

Klin tried to spin around to face his opponent. Cliff's grip on his leg kept him from facing his claws in the proper direction. The crab tried to reach, but lacked the flexibility. Nerves in his shell reached his brain. Blood began to trickle. Those huge pincers, the only weapon capable of breaching their shells, had successfully breached Klin's hide.

Green blood drizzled onto the ground.

Alas, the advantage of madness was limited. The poison in Cliff's veins was doing its wicked deed, shutting his internal organs down bit by bit. Muscle strength depleted, and with it, Cliff's grip on Klin's leg.

Klin pulled himself free, faced Cliff, and charged like a raging bull.

A clumsy mass of claws and legs flailed, each crab trying to pierce the other's shell. The brawl was ugly, both in the spillage of blood, but in their combat abilities. There was zero grace in the way they moved. There was no discipline, hardly any strategy, just a desire to disembowel each other.

Though sluggish, Cliff was not intent on losing. A snap of his claw got past Klin's guard and severed his left eye. The crab staggered back, suddenly half blind. Blood jetted from the stump of his eye stalk.

The new disability increased his sense of urgency. Desperate, and now experiencing a bout of madness of his own, Klin charged Cliff, grabbing his upper arms with both claws. Klin tilted Cliff upward, the latter's front legs kicking furiously as he was flipped onto his back.

Upside down, all eight legs were kicking, including the broken one. That did little to hinder Klin as he drove his claws into his opponent's underbelly. The shell, while durable against most threats, was powerless to withstand the power of crab pincers.

The claws penetrated Cliff's belly and peeled large flaps of shell. As the fragments parted, Cliff's soft insides were revealed to the world. Klin wasted no time shredding them. Like a fork separating a fresh package of ground beer, the pincers ripped back and forth. Gills, stomach, heart, bladder—it all became a soupy mixture, the shell serving as the bowl.

The legs stopped kicking, the claws lowering near Cliff's eyes. The crab was dead, killed by his lifelong companion.

"Hot damn," Jac muttered. As he watched the carnage unfold, he focused on the large crack in Klin's shell. "Rich, I think we've got ourselves an opportunity."

Richard knew exactly what he was referring to. "Foreman, you're up."

The bulking marine advanced several meters, took aim with his grenade launcher, and launched four explosives at the crustacean. Four consecutive blasts rocked the crab, widening the breach in his side.

Foreman turned left and ran, clearing the path for the rest of the marines.

"Weapons free," Richard said.

The three of them unleashed hell on the crab, the combined might of their blaster fire tearing up Klin's insides. The crab floundered in place, green blood and mist shooting from the gap in his shell. Only in Klin's final moments did he realize what was happening. By then, there was nothing he could do about it.

The crab slumped on his belly, his legs and arms sprawled out. He was motionless, aside from the river of green spilling from his shell.

Cliff and Klin were dead.

CHAPTER 17

The next several minutes were spent exchanging high fives with one another. In just a few minutes, fifty percent of the threat had been eradicated. Combined with Lance's death at the hands of the hawk eel, the team had only one crab to worry about.

"Well done," Jac said to the scientists. He slapped Milla and Foreman on the shoulder, then turned to face Richard. There was a pause as he searched for the right words to say, ultimately settling with, "Good call, Corporal."

It was enough for Richard.

"Thank you, Jac."

"Three down, one to go," Milla said.

"Who knows?" Ben added. "Maybe we might get out of this mess after all."

Sara grinned at the doctor. "Is that optimism I'm hearing?"

The group shared a laugh… then a collective gasp. The island, as though displeased with the humans' victory, knocked all seven of them to their knees with a mighty shake that could be felt for miles. The ocean rose and fell, smashing angrily into all four corners of the island.

A series of crunching and grinding could be heard behind the splashing of seawater.

CRACK! SPLASH!

A crevice formed near the hills, right behind the two dead crustaceans. As easily as crumbs falling from toasted bread, the entire south half of the island parted from the north. Breaking into enormous chunks, the land mass was swallowed by the swirling seas.

The shakes continued, chipping away at the north side. Richard glanced past the station at the north shoreline, hearing the splitting of rock and the crashing of water as the fragments broke away.

Relentlessly, the planet ate away at the island, stripping off more sections until that crevice behind the crabs widened. Forming a whole new shelf, several hundred meters of land shifted southwards, the dead crabs tumbling over the edge. The chunk of land split apart and descended into the waves.

As though momentarily satisfied, the planet eased its shaking into a mild tremor, reminding the survivors of what was to come.

Richard was back on his feet, observing his surroundings with astonishment. His world had shrunk by sixty percent. Only a little over two acres of land remained, holding the battered remains of Smith Station and the tower.

Ben, having fallen on his back during the quake, pushed himself to his hands and knees, flabbergasted at the recent event.

"Maybe I spoke too soon."

Under his palms, the island rumbled again, threatening to terrorize them with another catastrophic quake. All seven of them knew that one more earthquake of that scale would swallow the rest of the island.

"Up! Up!" Richard bellowed. "Everyone on your feet. Grab what you can; we're going to the boats. Jac, how much more work needs to be done patching up the hull?"

"More than I care to admit, but I'll rush it," Jac replied. He was on his feet, running east with John, Foreman, and Milla.

Richard ran inside with Sara and Ben, grabbed a couple large supply bags, then followed the others to the dock. Under each step, they felt the tectonic plates at war with each other. The ocean was like a growling stomach, ready to consume Smith Station and its inhabitants.

When they arrived at the docks, they found Jac and Foreman hurrying to get the next patch on.

"Hold it there," Jac said, pressing the flame to the edge of the sheet. He carefully worked his way down.

"We'll need another one right here," Foreman said, pointing to a crack in the hull just below the bottom edge of the sheet.

"Yes, I know that," Jac said.

John Kern was on the deck of the ship, eagerly awaiting departure. His face was a mixture of fright and disappointment.

This operation had come so close to greatness, only for Mother Nature to throw a curve ball at him. But he would come back. He needed to. His career depended on it. A new operation would be greenlit and, in all likelihood, John would be put in charge of the scientific regiment. He would go to the board and see to it they were equipped with floating facilities and more advanced watercrafts.

"How's it coming?" Richard said to Jac.

"Take a guess," Jac replied.

Richard put his supplies down, picked up a spare welding torch and patch sheet and stepped into the water with intent to cover a breach near the stern.

The crackling from the boat's radio brought him to a halt. He looked up at the ship's console, hearing the unmistakable sound of radio static. Within that static was a human voice.

"...*Station... .... Five-niner.... ... on approach... ...*"

Though they could barely make out what was being said, one thing was clear. Someone was nearing the planet's atmosphere, putting them in range of the boat's radio.

"Please tell me that's not my imagination," Ben said.

"No, that's real," John exclaimed. He hurried to the control console and adjusted the radio frequency. "Hello? This is Dr. John Kern, head science officer of Smith Station. Please repeat." More static came through. "Damn thing must've been rocked in the blast." He tried again to boost the signal.

Meanwhile, the others gathered near the bow, their collective anxiety now shifting back to sanguinity. The simple fact that someone was trying to make radio contact meant that Dante had successfully gotten a signal out.

"Dante, I hope God has made a special place in Heaven just for you," Richard said. He put his arm around Sara's shoulders and pulled her close.

"I'm confident He has," she said.

"They might not recognize the island," Foreman said. "Hell, considering the rate of decay, they might not even see it from high up."

"Do we have more flares?" Richard asked.

"Plenty," Sara replied.

"Then we'll flag them the old-fashioned way," Richard said. "They know the coordinates. If we shoot a flare, they'll see it."

"Hang on," John said. He was leaning over the console, tinkering with the knobs. "Might not have to worry about that. I might be able to get in contact with them after I fix this little—"

A wall of water burst from the ocean and splattered the shoreline, momentarily blinding the group. As the water pelted their faces, a crashing of metal filled the air. Then a scream.

When the water and mist subsided, the six people on shore beheld the sight of John Kern squirming in mid-air, a massive pincer closed over his midsection. The entire rear of the boat had been crushed, courtesy of Caesar, who had made his grand return to feast on the snack from beyond the stars.

John writhed in its grasp, pushing against the pincer in a vain attempt to force it open.

"No! No! NO!!!" This could not be happening. He was so close to freedom. He had a path to prosperity and wealth all figured out. He just needed to live!

A misty odor, containing the stench of previous victims, both humans and sea life, swept over him. He looked over his shoulder, seeing the large mandibles expand with intent to welcome him into the crab's gullet.

"NOOOO!!!"

That scream was quickly transformed into howls of agony, then the grunts of having his insides exposed to the world. What could have been over in a matter of seconds persisted for nearly a minute while Caesar relished the unique taste of human meat.

Dripping blood and bits of minced meat from his mouth, Caesar turned his big black eyes to the other six snacks on the shore.

Their only ride was gone along with the professor, leaving them with no other choice but to back away. An upsurge of anger came over the four marines, who began blasting away at the crustacean. Bullets made of hot energy barraged its shell, doing zero to deter the crab from coming after them.

Foreman, seeing the freshly cracked hull of the boat, took aim with his grenade launcher. All he needed was a well-placed shot to rupture the power cell and create a wall of chemicals that would maybe drive the crab backward.

He fired his four remaining grenades—right as the crab advanced. The explosives detonated uselessly on the living barrier. The crab halted momentarily from the force of the shockwaves. It was barely a minor inconvenience.

"Shit!" Foreman shouted, tossing his now-useless weapon to the ground.

"Back to the station!" Richard shouted.

Off they went, back the way they came, right to the very sanctuary that failed to protect the station's crew against the smaller crabs in hopes that it would somehow provide protection from Caesar. There was no time for planning and no effective weapons at their disposal. All they could do was hold out long enough for the dropship to arrive before the crab killed them all.

With that in mind, he looked at Sara. "Where's the flare pistol?"

"In the pack."

Richard slung his rifle over his shoulder and unzipped the pack, digging through it until he found the metal case. He opened it and removed the pistol and a fresh cartridge.

Hundreds of years of technological evolution, and here he was depending on one of the most primitive of human inventions to bring salvation.

He pointed the pistol skyward and squeezed the trigger. The bright red ball of fire soared high, its radiance capable of being seen for a two-mile radius. Hoping for the best, he tucked the pistol in his waist and led the group to the station.

Standing at the door, Richard opened fire on the oncoming crab. "Get in! Move! Move! Move!"

The survivors filed in, all of them retreating to the lab section of the building. Ben Cross, the last in line, dipped into the lounge, stopping a few steps inside to look at Richard.

"Come on, Corporal!"

His battery run dry, Richard dove inside. Directly behind him, a massive pincer slammed shut, missing his foot by inches. Scampering on all fours, Richard made his way further into the station.

Through those barricades, he and Ben saw the dark, bulky eyes staring back at them. In one explosive motion, the barricades burst from the walls, their busted fragments pelting them.

Caesar continued tearing away at the front of the station, eradicating any semblance of a structure. The claws reduced all four walls of the lounge area to pathetic, useless scraps, effortlessly closing in on the two humans who now stood in the hallway.

The crab continued forging a literal path of destruction, the claws now shredding the neck of the station, gradually working its way to the crew quarters and lab section.

Richard and Ben backed away, astonished to see the ceiling and walls imploding just a few feet in front of their eyes. No matter how fast they went, the destruction kept pace with them.

"Hurry it up, Corporal!" Milla shouted. She was in the lab, her machine gun mount hastily set up and pointed at the wall. Behind her, Sara, Jac, and Foreman stood ready, the latter now utilizing his Apone-86 submachine gun.

The marine and doctor turned and sprinted, both taking a right upon entering the lab. As soon as the line of fire was cleared, the group opened fire, forming a smoking river of energy at the crab.

The combined force of the projectiles was no more effective than had they been throwing cotton balls at the thing. Caesar kept coming, wading through the body of the station, his claws finally tearing out the south wall of the lab. Now in the large, open room, the crab could move a little more freely.

In this moment, they all realized hiding in this building was more useless than initially thought. At worst, they felt the structure would have bought them a few extra minutes, enough for them to maybe come up with a quick strategy. In fact, they may as well have taken refuge in a giant house of cards.

"Get back get back!" Richard shouted.

Caesar lunged at the firing line, the humans jumping back. The claw snapped shut, crushing Milla's machine gun. She backpedaled with the others toward the rear of the station, unslinging her submachine gun in the process.

The crab tossed the smashed weapon aside, gladly continuing the pursuit. The team dispersed, moving in separate directions across the lab.

"Here, take a bite of this!" Foreman shouted. He removed two grenades from his vest and tossed them at the crab.

Two explosions rocked the room, forcing everyone to cover their ears. Caesar leaned to the right, his left shoulder smoking from the impacts. Once the smoke cleared, the only evidence of Foreman's attack was some mild scarring on the shell.

Caesar turned, his attention now on the large marine. Clenching his teeth, Foreman knew in that moment his ticket was about to get punched. With too much debris between him and the back of the lab, retreat was not an option.

"Fuck…"

That was the only hint of a grievance. Taking the situation like a man, he pointed his weapon and unloaded it on the crab. Caesar waded through the blasts and snatched him in its claws. The pincer closed over his thighs, crushing the femurs as it lifted him from the floor.

It was now when Richard suspected this crab had some modicum of intelligence. The way it held Foreman in front of the others, it was not acting like a simple animal. It was sporting its catch, knowingly inflicting psychological warfare on the others. It knew what it was about to do next would drive the others to madness.

It held Foreman horizontally, then lined its other pincer up with him. It closed over his body, crushing his skull and cleaving him down the middle. The two halves, still held by the thighs in the other claw, were delivered to the mandibles.

The intended effect landed.

Milla shouted, both frightened and enraged. She blasted the crab with her weapon, the target slurping up her fellow marine while her shots went poof against its shell.

"Milla! Stop! Get back!" Richard shouted. She ignored the order, unloading her weapon on Caesar, who then approached.

Jac, realizing what was about to happen, grabbed her by the vest to pull her back.

The crab lunged, its target mostly out of reach. *Mostly.*

Milla fell on her back, feeling sudden warmth and wetness on her stomach. She looked down, seeing the gash across her abdomen.

"Oh... shit."

Seeing this, Jac scooped her up and turned to the north wall. "Hang on. We'll sew you back together. Just stay alive."

Milla stuffed a piece of fabric between her teeth and bit down. Groaning through the pain, she unholstered her pistol and fired at the big crab while Jac carried her off.

Realizing there was nowhere for his team to go, Richard turned his freshly reloaded gun to the north barricades. Several bolts punched through the welding patches, dropping the barricades and providing a clear path out of this death trap.

"Go! Get outside!"

Sara went for the exit, stopping to look back at Richard. He was several yards back, standing near the lab tables. "Richard!"

"Go! Jac! Get them out of here now. That's an order!"

Seeing the crab's attention on them, Jac did not hesitate to follow that order.

"Move it!" he said to Sara.

"But what about..."

"He'll be fine! If you don't move, we won't be!"

Her eyes welling, Sara hurried outside, laying down cover fire while the others filed out.

With the team out of the building, and the crab facing away from him, Richard committed to his makeshift plan. On the table in front of him was the last poison sac from the squid and the biopsy needle. He had watched how Ben Cross had done it before.

This was no time for caution. Sucking in a deep breath, he drove the syringe into the sac. To his amazement, the vial was filled with the purple contents.

"Hmm. No shit." Maybe in another life, he was a scientist or a physician. Or maybe he just had good luck. He hoped for the latter, because he was going to need it more than ever, considering the crazy shit he was about to attempt.

The crab was at the wall, ready to tear it down to continue chasing his friends. Richard looked at its back, then at its rear legs. One of them was firmly planted at a forty-five-degree angle, barely suitable as a ramp.

On the other side were the creature's relatively soft eyes.

"Oh, this is stupid," he muttered. He sprinted at the leg, running up its length onto the crab's back. Sensing his presence, Caesar turned around, nearly throwing the human off balance. Richard ran across its back, taking position atop of its head. Both claws lifted and bent, ready to snatch him off and pull him apart.

Right in front of him were the two eyes, bending backward to face him.

Richard grinned and brandished the needle. "Shouldn't have eaten my marines."

Holding the needle like a dagger, he drove it into Caesar's left eye, injecting every molecule of the squid's poison. The crab lurched, flinging him backward. Richard landed several feet behind the crab, hitting a mess of debris. Fighting against the dizziness and hazy vision, he sat up and scampered backward. His eyes were on the crab, which now turned around to face him. Its claws were sweeping across its eye, brushing away the irritating syringe that protruded from it.

Caesar's focus turned on the Corporal, the claws ready to tear him apart. Yet, the crab did not advance. This was not psychological warfare. It was not attempting to torture him with a demented sense of anticipation.

The way it slowly backed up, Richard knew it was unwell. The poison had gone straight into its bloodstream and was attacking the internal organs. The first thing to go was its appetite.

Bubbles formed at its mouth. The crab stumbled to the side, its legs seemingly struggling to keep it upright. An intense craving for water followed. Hearing the waves crash on the north shore, Caesar turned around, smashed through the wall, and retreated into the water.

Richard stood up just in time to see the crab disappear into the water. He stepped through the opening where the north wall had been, watching the water to make sure the creature did not reappear.

"Rich!" Sara sprinted at the Corporal, wrapping her arms around his neck. Before he could respond, he felt her lips press against his. There they remained for many good moments. "I thought you were dead."

"Not yet," he replied.
"It sure ran off in a hurry," she said. "What'd you do?"
Richard shrugged. "I poked it in the eye."

CHAPTER 18

"Hold still, Milla, or you'll make the incision worse," Jac said. He and Ben laid her down near the generator.

"How bad is it?" Milla asked.

Ben unclipped her vest and lifted her shirt for a better look at the laceration. She was literally split across the middle, her entrails threatening to fall right out. He gulped, cleared his throat, and forced a smile.

"Oh, you'll be fine… Practically a paper cut…"

Jac leaned over for a look, his face contorting into one of disgust and anxiety. He had seen more than his fair share of human anatomy. Seeing a complete stranger's insides was one thing. Seeing those of his friends, especially while she was still alive, was another thing entirely.

"A big ass paper cut," he muttered.

Milla groaned. "Doctor, I hope your medical skills are better than your lying."

Ben looked at Richard and Sara, his smile devolving into a nervous clenching of teeth. "Corporal! You're alive. Miracles never cease."

"What happened? We saw the crab run off," Jac said.

"Managed to hit it with a dose of squid poison," Richard said.

"No shit?!" Jac exclaimed. "How much? Is it dying?"

"Your guess is as good as mine," Richard said. "Got a partial syringe-full in its eye."

"Considering its size, we can't know for certain," Sara said. "Fortunately, it was enough to drive it away for the short term."

Milla's shouting put the conversation to an end. Ben gritted his teeth, digging his hand into the incision.

"Sorry, Marine. I gotta do this… there!" He looked up at Richard. "I found one of the bleeders. I'm pinching it shut, but I need my equipment."

Richard looked at the wreckage that was once Smith Station. Only some of the lab section remained standing.

"Holy shit. Doctor, not only will I not know what I'm looking for, I'm not sure I'd be able to find it in all that mess."

Looking at the wreckage, Ben realized the Corporal had a point. That did not change the dynamics of the situation. He needed his tools now, or Milla would bleed to death. He did not have the luxury of explaining the equipment and where exactly it was located. Plus, there was the question of whether or not it was functional.

"Sara! I need you to pinch this bleeder," he said. "Keep it shut until I get back."

Sara knelt down. "Sorry, Milla. This is gonna hurt." She winced, not enjoying the sensation of human entrails while she reached into the wound. She found the severed vein and squeezed it shut.

Ben stood up. "Come on, Corporal. I'll need your help."

The two men sprinted for the lab.

"What exactly are we grabbing?" Richard asked.

"My bio scanner and my auto-surgical kit," Ben said. "Does most of my job for me. I just need to type in the right codes."

They entered the lab, stopping momentarily after seeing the devastation inside. It was a striking sight, seeing through the lab to the other side of the island, with no hallway or lounge in the way. The entire south half of the building had caved in on itself after Caesar had come raging through like an armored bull. The lab wasn't much better. The floor had been ripped up by Caesar's eight feet. Much of the machinery was knocked over and reduced to fragments. There was no power for the little equipment that survived the assault. The lights had switched off, the only light coming from the sun. Pieces of the ceiling dangled, ready to come apart at a moment's notice.

"Where's the infirmary?" Richard said, looking at the pile of debris.

"Down this way," Ben said. He turned right and went down the little pathway near the refrigerator unit, right where the marines had first encountered the mantids. He went into the room at the end of the hall and immediately cursed. "Shit! SHIT! Oh, shit!"

"What's the matter?" Richard asked. He followed Ben into the infirmary, the imploded ceiling serving as an answer to his question. The shockwaves from the crab's rampage had caused much of the room to cave in on itself, damaging much of the equipment inside.

The two men frantically dug through the debris, tossing bits of ceiling and wall to the side.

"What does this bio-scanner look like?" Richard said.

Ben sat up and groaned. "This." He held up a damaged tablet-shaped machine. It was cracked down the middle, having taken a heavy hit during the wreckage. He tried to get it to work, to no avail. He tossed it aside, then suppressed a scream as his eyes looked at something across the room.

Across from him was a fairly large object, tan in color, resembling a large briefcase. Richard could tell it was mechanical in nature, designed to unfold and perform some kind of medical purpose. It was on its side, the upper portion heavily cracked and cratered.

Ben hurried over to it and tried opening it. He managed to get it to unfold, which only led to his fears being confirmed. The inside contained several mechanical arms and scanners, all designed to perform complex surgical operations. The scanners and screens in the computer sections were cracked and dark.

"I'm guessing that's the auto-surgical kit," Richard said.

"Yes." Ben spoke in a low whisper, staring at the busted machinery with a monotonous languor. He was frozen in place, more terrified now than when retreating from a monster crab. A tense awareness had set in, one that shook Ben Cross to his very core.

Looking at his face, Richard's intuition kicked in. He knew why the doctor was frightened.

"You're gonna have to perform the surgery yourself, Doctor."

"Yes, but I…"

"Do you have the tools you need to stop the bleeding and stitch her together?"

"Yes, but…"

"No buts, Doctor!" Richard grabbed Ben by the shoulders and smacked him lightly on the face to shock him out of his indecisive state. "Get it together, Dr. Cross. You're Milla's only hope. We can't waste time mourning over a busted piece of technology. You know what to do. So, you screwed up in the past. So have I. What matters is what you do now. Now... what do we need to grab?"

Ben took a long deep breath and exhaled. It was as though he was expelling his fears and uncertainties out of his mind, gradually getting his game face on. He knew Richard was right. Though he was afraid he would screw up, he knew giving in to fear and letting Milla bleed to death would be worse than failure.

He stood up and went to a large steel container on the west side of the room. He opened the doors and started handing Richard IV units, tubing, a scalpel kit, and a metal device with a long, narrow neck.

"Go out there. I'll get the rest," he said. As Richard turned around, Ben pulled out a suture kit and a suction device, then raced outside.

The two men knelt beside Milla, the doctor putting on a medical facemask and gloves before leaning over the wound.

"Where's the auto-surgical kit?" Sara asked.

"Damaged," Ben said. He applied the IV line to Milla's arm, Jac holding the bag up for them. Ben switched on the suction device, pushing the base toward Richard while he took the end of the hose to the wound. "Alright, I'm gonna remove a little blood. She's already lost quite a bit. She'll need a transfusion once this is done."

"We're the same type," Jac said.

"That's fortunate," Ben said. "Hope you're volunteering, because she'll need it."

"We'll worry about that afterward," Richard said.

Ben went to work, removing some of the blood and getting a better look at the damage inside. "Alright, hold still Milla. I'm gonna cauterize this vein..." He took the funny-looking device from Richard and extended the narrow end into the wound. The tip ignited a tiny spark, sealing the vein and stopping the blood loss.

Next, he went through his suture kit, then lowered some stitches into the wound. Slowly and carefully, he began patching up some of the internal damage. He started with the tear in the stomach tissue, slowly applying a stitch. Large droplets of sweat formed on his hairline. Ben swallowed, willing himself to soldier through the anxiety and keep his hands steady. Weaving the thin, bio-degradable thread, he successfully sealed Milla's stomach back up. He identified another bleeder, cauterized it, then removed his instruments from the wound.

"Nice work, Milla. Still with us?"

"I swear, if we survive this, I'm gonna host Crab Fest every Friday," Milla said.

"Am I invited?" Ben asked.

"As long as I don't die."

Ben chuckled. "Just stay awake, and you'll be fine. The worst part is over. I'm stitching your gut together now."

"Gut?" she groaned. "What are you saying there, Doc?"

The group laughed. It was a relief for everybody to see that wound close up. Ben Cross applied the stitches, his breathing now steady, the self-loathing cloudiness gone from his eyes.

"Well done, Doctor," Richard said.

Ben looked at him and nodded. "That's my job, Corporal."

Richard took the IV bag while Ben prepped Jac for a blood transfusion. He transferred roughly a unit of blood from him to Milla, taking her blood pressure afterwards.

"She's stable for now. Still needs a proper hospital bed," Ben said.

"There's one on the freighter," Richard said. He looked to the sky. "If only we had a ride that'll get us there."

Turning every which way, he scanned the horizon in hopes of seeing white contrails from a dropship. It had to be near. They were in range of the boat's radio for god sake.

Adding insult to injury, the ground began to shift. The ocean came alive, throwing its usual fit on what remained of the island. Layers of granite deep beneath their feet cracked loudly, signaling that the island was ready to split into numerous pieces and come apart.

"Seems we can't catch a break," Sara said.

"Maybe…" Ben looked to Richard, then at the flare pistol he carried. "Maybe not."

Richard took the hint. After loading a fresh cartridge into the pistol, he pointed it high and fired.

Maybe, God willing, the dropship was close enough to see it.

They watched the ball of flame reach its maximum height of one thousand feet then slowly arch downward, falling eastward like a burning meteor. Down it went, striking the ocean, its flames still sparkling as it vanished under the waves.

A deep, thunderous crack vibrated through the island.

All five survivors looked to the west, seeing the hill and radio tower peel into the water, leaving a jagged rock shelf in its wake. As the shakes continued, more pieces followed, the 'shoreline' slowly making its way toward the inhabitants.

Richard opened the gun and pulled the last cartridge from the case. One last shot. One last hope.

"Third time's the charm…" He pointed the pistol high, ready to squeeze the trigger.

"Wait!" Sara put a hand on his arm, stopping him. "Listen."

Through the crashing of waves, they heard the humming of engines. They looked to the south, finally seeing that white stream.

The dropship's vertical thrusters kicked in, slowing its approach. Spotting the group of humans, the pilot steered it near the station. Finding the flattest area of land available, it set down.

"Hot damn," Milla said in a strained voice.

Richard passed the IV bag to Sara. "Get Milla ready. I'll be right back. I gotta make sure these guys are ready for a fast takeoff." He took a few quick steps toward the dropship.

"Corporal?"

Richard stopped and looked back at Jac. After removing the transfusion needle from his arm, Jac hurried over to the Corporal.

"Yes?" Richard said.

Jac let out a sharp exhale, the only hesitation he could allow himself before admitting the truth.

"No other way to put it," Jac said. "Going after the shuttle… you were right and I was wrong. Had things gone my way, we'd be underwater long before we got that tower up and running. You did good."

The two men clasped arms.

"Don't worry about it," Richard said. "Help Milla onto the ship. Then we can finally say goodbye to this Godforsaken place."

"Yes sir, Corporal," Jac said.

The two men parted ways. Richard sprinted to the ship's ramp, which was already dropping. A crewmember stood behind it, visibly flabbergasted after seeing the island's condition.

"Corporal?" the crewman said. "Where's Sergeant Walker?"

"Dead," Richard said. "I'll explain later. First, we're gonna need to take off ASAP. We've got an injured marine who needs immediate medical attention."

"You got it," the crewman said.

Richard looked back, seeing Jac, Ben, and Sara lifting Milla off the ground. Slowly, they approached, struggling to keep their balance as the island continued to shake.

"Something tells me you have a hell of a story to tell," the crewman said.

"You don't know the half of it," Richard replied.

Adding to his point, the ship's alarm went off. The ramp started cranking back up, catching both men by surprise.

"The hell?! What's going—" Richard shut his jaw, catching the sound of drumming feet rapidly approaching. The dropship's vertical thrusters went to work, performing an emergency lift off. As it moved from view, Richard's worst fear was realized.

Darting in from the east shore was Caesar. The damn crab was still alive and ready to finish his reign of terror. There was a sluggishness in his movements, the poison having caused some internal damage. Despite this, the crab was not willing to let his human snacks escape.

Caesar lifted his claws at the ship, which was now far out of reach. A door gunner took position, blasting away at the crab. As expected, the blasts did nothing but agitate the crab further.

"Oh, Lord!" Jac exclaimed. "Get back, everybody."

"To where?!" Sara exclaimed.

The ship began to circle around in search of another place to land. Except there was no other suitable place to land. On top of that, the island was shrinking before their very eyes. Part of the north shore broke away, putting the waterline just a few feet ahead of the station.

Huge cracks took form, stretching from shore to shore. The survivors glanced at the ground, which was at best minutes away from splitting, then at the big crab which was preventing their only means of escape from landing.

Richard sneered at Caesar. His patience had run out. This crab and his little brethren had caused him and his friends enough trouble for one day. No longer was this a question of survival. For Richard Carson, this was now personal.

"You wanna fight?!" He marched toward the crab, blasting away with his rifle. Feeling the heat of plasma bolts hitting its shell, the crab turned to face him. "Huh? This what you want? A good fight? I'll give ya one." He aimed for the crab's eyes, managing to singe one of the stalks before the claws rose over them.

Richard kept firing until the battery ran out. Giving in to his newfound rage, he threw the weapon at the crab.

Caesar parted his claws, watching the gun smash against his arm. Richard successfully had its attention.

He wasn't done. He unholstered his pistol and fired off several shots.

Caesar moved on him, claws open. He was ready to kill Richard, not only to feed, but out of retaliation for the injury he had received in the lab.

"Get on the ship! GO!" Richard shouted at the others. Without giving them a chance to respond, he sprinted south, with Caesar right behind him.

"Richard, NO!" Sara yelled.

It was too late. The Corporal was committed, leading the crab to the south end of the island, clearing the landing zone for the dropship.

The pilot kept the ship in the air for a few more seconds, monitoring the chase and confirming no other threats were in the area. He set it down again and lowered the ramp a second time.

The crewman was standing by, immediately waving the survivors aboard.

"Move it! Come on!"

"What about Richard?" Sara said.

Jac watched as one of the cracks began to widen. "We'll get him. First, let's get aboard before we fall through this thing."

They carried Milla aboard, the crewman wheeling an IV pole over to her. As they strapped her in, they watched the series of cracks expand, the various segments of land gradually parting ways.

"Pilot! Take off!" the crewman said. He held on to a grab bar while the dropship lifted off.

"We're not leaving without Richard," Sara said.

"We might have to," the crewman said.

"Like hell we do," Jac said.

The crewman sighed. "Do we even know where he is?"

Ben put his eyes to one of the viewing ports, spotting a big crab running southward.

"Yep! That way!"

CHAPTER 19

One moment, Richard was running straight. The next, he was running on a downward slope. The stretch of island ahead, which previously had been hilly, was now crumbling before his very eyes. The mounds broke into small pebbles, which rolled down their slopes and disappeared into the many various cracks that formed across the deteriorating landscape.

A miniature apocalypse was reaching its conclusion, resulting in Challenger's oceans covering even more of its surface. Beneath it all, the plates were shifting, further obstructing the Titanus-mons fluid that John Kern and the Assembly so desperately wanted to exploit. Perhaps there would be more visits to this planet. The Assembly was not one to give up easily, but then again, neither did Challenger. It had repelled the first human settlement using only a few crabs and earthquakes. Richard could only imagine what other secrets lay beneath those deceptively welcoming waters.

Repelled. That was what it felt like as he was chased. No doubt, Caesar had every desire to eat him, probably after cutting him up into several pieces just for good measure. But even as he ran for dear life, Richard could not shake the feeling that there was more to this planet than underwater earthquakes and hungry sea monsters. Maybe it was God's way of preserving something special. Or maybe it was the opposite. Maybe he was warning mankind against something horrible. Perhaps, even after all the tragedies that led up to now, it was possible that He was actually doing humans a favor. After all, just because something looked beautiful, did not mean it was good.

Who'd ever guess my thought process while being chased by a crab as big as a trailer would be philosophical instead of "Holy shit, I'm being chased by a crab as big as a trailer!"?!

Every vein in Richard's neck bulged as he felt the crab closing in behind him. Less than thirty feet ahead of him was the south shore. Twenty feet, actually, as a ten-foot section peeled off as he ran toward it.

Caesar was undeterred by the turbulence. The crab had lived on this planet all of its life and experienced nature's wrath in more ways than one. The demise of this island was just another day in its life as far as it was concerned. If there was any downside, it was the fact that Challenger was going to run out of its new favorite snack.

In the few seconds he had before running out of space, Richard dropped his pistol and yanked the flare gun from his waist. He could hear the dropship's engines far back. His friends were saved, his mission complete. Whether he survived was unimportant, so long as he managed to get the survivors out of harm's way.

Still, he had no intention of going out without a fight. After all, Caesar did kill John Kern and two of his teammates and had nearly killed Milla. It had tried to kill the others, including Sara, and now it was trying to kill Richard. Hell, it wouldn't even let them escape from this planet. Whether it did so out of malice or predatory instinct was irrelevant. Richard had a bone to pick with Caesar, and he would see it through.

"Alright, you walking seafood feast, if you're gonna eat me, you're gonna have to commit!" That last word was screamed as Richard leapt into the water. Hands forward like a professional diver, he plunged at a sixty-degree angle. The blue waters were now grey with a mix of sediment.

Caesar accepted the challenge, his big mass creating a tidal wave as he splashed down after the human.

Even if it hadn't jumped, the crab would have been in the water anyway, for another large section of land broke apart. Richard looked behind him, seeing the island now forming an underwater mountain. The crab was only ten feet deep, walking along the new slope.

Looking straight down, Richard realized that the bottom was only a few feet under him. Knowing the crab couldn't swim, he hoped he could get out far enough to where Caesar would be too deep to reach him. From there, he would plan his next attack. As luck would have it, doing so would be harder than he thought.

A lot harder.

A dash of motion stopped Richard in place. Looking through the thin clouds of silt, he noticed a few figures buzzing around like bees.

Oh, heil, not those freaking mantids again!

There were at least a half dozen of them in sight. As usual, the starving creatures were in constant search for anything they could snack on. It wasn't long before they detected Richard's movements.

One of them turned in his direction, and without delay, it shot right toward him.

Richard lifted his head above the water's surface, taking a much-needed breath while unsheathing his combat knife. Ducking back down, he stared through the salty water at the four-foot predator.

Bring it.

He thrust both feet out, hitting the thing as it closed in. Caught off guard by the impact, the mantid wheeled to its left, its legs thrashing violently, trying to regain position and momentum. Like wrestling an alligator, Richard threw himself onto the thing, locking his legs around its abdomen to hold it close as he drove the knife into its head. The mantid spasmed, then went stiff. Richard unlocked his legs, letting the dead crustacean descend to its watery grave.

It wasn't but two seconds when he lifted his gaze before another one came at him. This one managed to make contact, driving him backward... right toward the shallower portion of the now sunken island.

Feeling its forelegs dig into his hips, Richard stabbed at the thing frantically. The thin shell over its head was no match for the cold steel of his knife. The tip of the blade found its brain, cutting its attack short. The mantid's forelegs parted, releasing the marine. Kicking the creature away, he moved to the surface and took a deep breath.

He looked to the north, just in time to see the rest of the island split apart. The water simmered, swallowing the only bit of land for miles. Only a few feet underneath, the remnants settled, forming a perfect cone-shaped structure.

Having been pushed closer to its tip, Richard was now in less than ten feet of water. All Caesar needed to do was make his way over to him, and the marine would be within reach—a fact the crab clearly recognized. It was several yards to the west, moving in his direction.

To the south, those mantid creatures continued to congregate, many of them locating the marine with their antennae. They swam along the surface in a tight race.

Richard breathed softly, keeping himself from succumbing to panic. He knew when he led the crab away that death was likely. Now, death seemed not only likely, but certain. All he could control was whether or not he died a good death. A warrior's death.

He held the knife in a reverse grip and waited for the bastards to approach.

Alright. Who's next?

Ion engines droned overhead, the vertical thrusters sending ripples into the ocean. Next came clouds of vapor as hot plasma rained down onto the swarm. Mantid creatures darted in all directions, many of them tossing and turning after being struck.

Looking up, Richard saw the dropship. At the door gun was Jac, muttering a few catch phrases which were drowned out by the engines and gunfire.

The swarm turned back and retreated into open water. Even the ones that were several feet underwater darted away, despite being safe from the projectiles. At first, Richard figured they were following the swarm. He doubted they swam off out of fear of the gun, especially if the plasma bullets fizzled out as soon as they touched the water.

Then he remembered the only other thing the mantids feared.

Richard looked down.

"SHIT!"

Caesar's claw was right below him, wide open, ready to close around his groin. The marine threw himself to the side, thrusting and kicking with all his might. The claw shut, the tips finding his shin. Muscle split, shinbone cracked, and Richard yelled. Knowing he was less than a moment from being pulled down, he took a quick gasp, then shut his jaw.

The crab pulled him to the sea bottom. Richard was on his back, lying on the mountain slope as though on a slab, staring at the mad beast. Its claw was still clamped over his leg, keeping him in place.

Caesar seemed to admire his catch before butchering it, as though relishing the fact that he had finally beat this very troublesome human.

The other claw opened and shut repeatedly, demonstrating the agony it was about to put Richard through. By now, the marine no longer wondered if this thing was a mindless beast. Nope, it had a degree of intelligence. Not only intelligence, but malevolence. It had its prey at its mercy, without any weapons to use against it. Not that the weapons did any serious harm. Caesar lowered its claw to dice Richard. A truly wicked creature, it knew exactly what it was doing.

Unfortunately for it, so did Richard.

He pulled the pistol from his waist and fired point blank into Caesar's eye. The crab released the marine, darting back several yards, its claws brushing at the annoying flame that blinded it.

A bright red light, it was capable of being seen for miles, drawing the attention of predators near and far. Especially near.

Within seconds, Richard spotted the snake-like figure swimming in from the southwest. Drawn by the light, the hawk eel went directly for Caesar. It was undeterred by the crab's massive size and weaponry. Territorial, it was ready to kill and eat any competition that wandered into the area.

Parting its huge beak, the eel sprang into action. The jaws found Caesar's rear leg and bit down over the center joint. Still flustered with the flare in its eye, the crab reeled backward, surprised by the sudden igniting of nerves in its leg. It leaned back, then tried to turn around.

The eel tightened its grip, cracking the shell, making an exit for a cloud of green blood. Caesar spun about, trying to grab at the attacker, his eye still ablaze thanks to that annoying flare.

Like a massive python, the eel began slipping its tail around the crab's body, hoping to hold it in place while the beak gradually cut through the shell. The jaws squeezed even tighter.

Crack!

The leg parted, falling stub-over-tip down the slope of the mountain, trailing a thin mist of green blood. Before the severed limb settled, it was met by a swarm of hungry mantids, who crowded at the open stub to get at the meat inside.

Meanwhile, the fight continued, the eel now searching for a new place to bite.

Richard scooted back, holding his breath as best he could. He had a minute of air left. Though he was only eight or nine feet deep, he may as well have been a hundred. His left leg was thoroughly broken, forcing his other limbs to work overtime in order to get to the surface.

With no other option, he groaned through the pain and swam.

"I don't see him," the pilot shouted through the cockpit door.

"No visual from port quarter section," the crewman said.

Ben and Sara moved from one viewing port to the next, desperately trying to get a visual on Richard.

"He was right there a minute ago," Jac said from the door gun.

"He was grabbed by the thing," the pilot said. "I'm sorry, Marine, but it looks like the Corporal is K.I.A. We're gonna have to go."

Jac unharnessed himself from the door gun and made his way straight to the cockpit, hand on his sidearm. The pilot and co-pilot's eyes went wide, sensing the marine's potentially violent determination.

"I dare you to abandon him. Go ahead. See what happens."

The pilots looked at each other, internally debating whether to argue, resist, or resume searching. They went with the last option, which quickly turned out to be the correct one.

"There he is!" Sara said, pointing to starboard.

The pilots turned the vessel, spotting him.

"Lower the ramp, I'll toss the rescue harness," Jac said. He ran aft, relieved to see that the crewman had the line prepped and ready to go. Jac had only known this guy for five minutes, but he liked him already.

The ship lowered to ten feet. Richard was on the surface, clearly in pain and struggling to keep his head above water. Behind him, two monstrous shapes tussled along the mountainside, their motions causing a whole new series of violent waves.

"Corporal!" Jac shouted. Richard swam toward him, only to stop and turn to the right. Jac put his arms out. "What are you doing? Why'd you st—" The answer came in the form of several insectoid shapes converging once again on Richard. "Damn, those pests! They're everywhere!"

The two marines shouldered plasma rifles and blasted away at the small horde. Sara pulled another rifle from the rack and joined in. The combined heat of their attack successfully drove the swarm apart. Those who were hit foundered, the others darting away. Only one committed to the attack, coursing through the bombardment, tackling Richard to the seabed.

"No!" Sara shouted.

"Damn it!" Jac exclaimed.

"What happened?" Ben asked. "Did they get him? Don't tell me he's dead!"

"No way," Milla moaned. "It's gonna take more than a mantid to kill Richard Carson."

Jac and Sara remained at the ramp, waiting for the Corporal to prove that point.

The thing dug its sharp forelegs into its side, its swimmerets pushing him right back against the mountain slope.

Richard was more pissed than hurt, for he was sick of being forced underwater, as well as being trapped on this planet. He pushed against the mantid's neck, keeping its jaws at bay.

Mandibles stretched and coiled, trying to scrape even the slightest bit of flesh from his body. Instead, they tasted the cold edge of his knife.

Richard pushed the blade through its mouth, the blade coming out the back of its head. He pushed the creature off and rested for a moment, the pain in his leg pulsing through his entire body. Up above, a few of the mantid creatures darted about. He had no doubt they saw him, but were too afraid to commit, as the crab and eel were literally three yards to his right. All they wanted was for him to swim to the surface, just far enough where they were comfortable to grab him and pull him away from the two giants.

I'm really getting fed up with this bullshit!

He turned his eyes to the fight. The eel was constricting Caesar, having successfully bitten off a second leg. With its balance shifting, the crab teetered to the right, ultimately rolling onto its belly.

The eel seized the opportunity, sinking its beak through the slits of the underbelly. Like a woodpecker, it hammered the tip into the belly, gradually chipping away with unimaginable force. Caesar kicked his legs and slashed with claws, finding nothing but water.

The eel angled its head and parted its jaws, slipping the lower jaw into the stub where the rear leg had been. Like scissors, the beak closed, the top part applying pressure to the underbelly.

Crack!

A fault line worked its way down the crab's stomach. Moving down the breach, the eel bit again.

Crack!

The breach widened, the crab's shell threatening to slip open entirely. Blood spilled out from the big wide wound.

Nerves went haywire, overloading Caesar's brain. Throwing all of its weight to the left, the crab did the impossible. It righted itself.

The sudden change of motion caused the eel's tail to strike a sharp piece of rock, forcing it to uncoil from around the crab's shoulder. Caesar snapped with two powerful claws, securing a painful grip on its end.

Now, it was the eel who was experiencing a flood of pain. Separating its jaws from the belly, the eel attacked the pincers, hoping to crush them under its beak and free itself.

This course of action proved to be the eel's downfall. Caesar opened one of his claws and grabbed the eel by the throat, the edges cutting flesh. Holding it by the front and back, he watched as the eel squirmed, suddenly helpless after nearly achieving victory.

Its death was slow and unceremonious. Caesar tightened the left claw, feeling the splitting of flesh under his grip. There was the satisfying reverberation of vertebrae cracking, followed by the parting of the eel's head.

Red blood mixed with the clouds of green and gray, reducing the sight of the crab to a mere silhouette. That did not stop Caesar from remembering his original intentions.

Richard watched that silhouette drop the eel carcass. Slowly, it moved through the silt and fluid, straight towards him. The crab's movements were sluggish, the injuries taking a toll, but not enough to deter it from the satisfaction of slaughtering him.

The marine flinched, caught off guard by the sudden appearance of one of the mantid creatures. Oddly, the relatively small creature seemed to have no problem swimming close to the crab, which its species usually avoided like the plague.

Another one appeared. Then another.

Caesar stopped, equally as perplexed by the sudden proximity of these lesser lifeforms.

Three became six. Six became twelve. Twelve became a hundred and twenty!

In the blink of an eye, they were everywhere, circling Caesar and the dead eel. Some of them converged on the dead giant, gladly feasting on the soft flesh. The others kept their attention on the crab, with many moving in from behind.

New pain surged through his body. The crab lurched, feeling the crack in his shell widening as a dozen bodies forced themselves inside all at once. Entering through the crack on its underside, the mantids found their way to the soft flesh, immediately helping themselves to mouthfuls at a time.

Overloaded with unbearable pain, Caesar started to spin. Those big claws lashed at the horde, managing to pluck one mantid and rip it apart. The effort meant little in the long run, as a hundred of the things converged on its wounds.

The crab could feel little bodies moving inside of its own, ripping through muscle and organ tissue. Like ants, they scurried about, some of them literally walking on the inside of its shell.

Losing balance again, Caesar rolled onto his back. There, the titan of the sea could do nothing while he was eaten alive from the inside by countless starving mantids who, until two minutes ago, feared the beast. Until his weakness was discovered, that is.

Despite his lungs begging for air, Richard could not help but watch the feeding frenzy with a strange fascination. In this moment, he thought of Sara, and the rare spectacle the marine biologist was missing out on.

Directly above him, the rescue harness hit the water. With seconds to go, the marine made his way to the surface. With the mantid colony busy with devouring Caesar and the eel, he had a clear path.

Feeling the luxury of air once again, Richard rewarded his lungs.

"There he is!" Jac shouted. "Corporal! Grab onto the line."

Richard was already on it. Securing the harness around his waist and shoulders, he gave a thumbs up to the crew. They winched him in, Jac and Sara helping him onto the ramp.

"Uh-oh," Ben said, looking at the way Richard hobbled. "Broken leg. What the hell happened down there? Get in a brawl with Caesar?"

Richard smirked, relishing the feeling of steel beneath his feet.

"Yeah, you can say that," he said.

"Did you win?" Jac said, smacking him on the shoulder.

Richard cocked his head in the direction of the feeding frenzy. "With a little help."

They shared a laugh as they helped the Corporal to a seat. The ramp closed, the pilots elevating the aircraft to avoid any other surprises.

"Here, keep your leg elevated," Ben said.

"How's it looking, Doctor?" Jac asked.

"Eh, it's busted up pretty good," Ben said. "But I've seen worse. Get me into a proper infirmary, I'll have him and Milla looking good as new."

"I'll hold you to that," Sara said, taking a seat beside Richard.

Milla smirked, planting a cigar between her teeth. "Oh, I think the doc can handle it."

"Damn right." Jac took a seat between Richard and Milla and strapped himself in. With everyone secured, the pilots took the ship high into the atmosphere. Before long, they were looking at a wide scope of ocean, then the spherical shape of Challenger as they entered space.

Sara closed her eyes, feeling the sanctuary from danger for the first time in days. Nothing felt better than resting her head on Richard's shoulder and appreciating the things she had nearly lost.

"Hell of a day," Richard said.

"What happens from here?" Sara asked.

"Well, in the short term, after the infirmary, it'll be back to the cryopods. Then back to Fort Matthews, straight to my hearing, I suppose." Richard shut his eyes and enjoyed her company. After what they had all been through, he could hardly care less about his demotion. Five of their marines were dead, men he had known for years. Compared to that, a hearing seemed like child's play.

Despite all of that, there was one shining light in the darkness. That light sat beside him, leaning against his shoulder.

Jac scoffed. "Hearing? What hearing?" He made a 'tisk' sound and shook his head. "I might have to send Fort Matthews a message and set them straight. They'll need to be updated on what just occurred, anyway."

"Yeah," Milla said. "Once they read the report, they might have a different opinion of you by the time we get home."

Richard smiled and opened his eyes. Holding an elevated appreciation for his friends, new and old, he turned his eyes to the viewing port for one last glimpse of the planet Challenger.

"Whatever happens, I'm just happy not to set foot on that damn ball ever again," he said.

"Challenger," Sara said. "I guess it lived up to the name."

Richard shook his head. "Should've called it Crustacean Planet."

The team enjoyed a laugh. Together, they watched the planet disappear from view.

Made in United States
North Haven, CT
08 August 2023